CADILLAC CHRONICLES

CADILLAC CHRONICLES

BY BRETT HARTMAN

CINCO PUNTOS PRESS
www.cincopuntos.com

FIRST EDITION
10 9 8 7 6 5 4 3 2 1

Library of Congress Cataloging-in-Publication Data

Hartman, Brett, 1964-
  Cadillac chronicles / by Brett Hartman.
     p. cm.
Summary: Without his mother's knowledge or approval, sixteen-year-old Alex takes a road trip with Lester, an elderly black man in the adopt-a-senior program, to find Alex's father in Fort Lauderdale.
  Cloth ISBN 978-1-935955-41-2 (alk. paper); e -book ISBN 978-1-935955-42-9
  [1. Friendship—Fiction. 2. Old age—Fiction. 3. Fathers—Fiction. 4. African Americans—Fiction. 5. Automobile travel—Fiction.] I. Title.

  PZ7.H26726Cad 2012
  [E]—dc23   2012019961

Book and cover design by Antonio Castro H.
Going to D.F. to talk about covers and collaboration.

Thanks to Harry Durgan for the cover photo of Brett Hartman. Thanks also to good old friend Cephus (Dusty) Rhodes and the handsome Christian Pleters along with his father Michael for sitting through the photo shoot (of sorts) for the cover of *Cadillac Chronicles*. And to the incomparable H&H Carwash for hosting that event. And to the beautiful girl who walked into Cinco Puntos Press and got her photo taken, but whose phone number I lost. Oh well. Great cover, isn't it? We can't forget Vicky Smith who is forever keeping her eye on the world of small presses! We're still blushing.

In memory of Rebecca Riley
April 11, 2002—December 13, 2006

CHAPTER ONE

Alex Riley walked the lower level of the Tri-City Mall while his roving eyes did what they were prone to do — scope out female body parts. And the mall didn't disappoint. A late spring heat wave had turned the place into a festival of cleavage. It would have been the perfect way to spend a Saturday evening. Except for one annoying detail. His mother was walking next to him, stride for stride. Their mission was to get him a replacement pair of high-top sneakers, and she was all business.

"There it is," she said, pointing to the illuminated storefront. "Then we're going home."

Alex unscrewed the cap from his Dr. Pepper. "Why don't we do the circuit?" he said. "The whole mall, for exercise?"

"I've already treadmilled three miles and my hair's a mess. Let's just pick out the shoes and go."

"You could get your hair done while I walk the mall."

"Alex, please don't test my patience." She remained at the store entry while he surveyed a wall of sneakers. There were dozens of styles, but only one he really wanted. He spotted it mid-level near the cash register. Black leather with understated swooshes. He flipped the shoe and admired it from all angles. Prized sneaker in hand, he stepped toward his mother while she busily worked the keypad on her phone. "Is that what you want?" she said without lifting her eyes from the screen.

"Excuse me, Patricia?" said a lanky man in a blue crew sweater. "Thought that was you."

Her head popped up at the man's voice. "Commissioner," she said. "It's great to see you." Her arm gave a little tremble as she pocketed her phone.

"Great to see you too." The man looked at Alex. "Who do we have here?"

She reached for Alex's arm and pulled him close. "Commissioner, this is my son Alex. Alex, this is Commissioner Holcombe."

Alex nodded while gulping the last of his soda.

"How do you do, Alex?" The man extended a gaunt hand, tufts of gray hair at the knuckles like miniature welcome mats.

Alex shook the commissioner's hand. But then he couldn't stop himself. The soda had prompted a full-throttled burp, and there was no free hand to cover his mouth. It came out loud and raw. Centered on his tongue was a knob of silver mounted on a post.

His mother gasped. "I am so sorry, Commissioner."

"It's quite all right." The man winked at Alex. "It's called being a teenager." He looked back at Patricia. "I'll see you at the office."

"Yes, yes, that'll be great." She tightened her grip on Alex's arm. With her free hand she waved goodbye.

Once the commissioner was far enough away, she glared at Alex. "You ungrateful pig! You have any idea who that is?"

He hadn't really thought about it, but the answer was obvious.

His mother was deputy commissioner of Albany County, so the man was probably a rung or two up the political ladder. And she was the climbing type. She wouldn't get a decent night's rest until she reached the top step, looking down at everybody else. She went on talking, almost yelling: "If you think you're getting those sneakers, you're living in a fantasy world!"

"Sorry mom, but he didn't care. He even winked at me."

"I don't care if he hugged you. What you did was totally uncalled for."

Alex noticed a pack of kids at a sunglasses kiosk smiling and staring right at him. "Mom, you're making a scene."

"Put down the shoe," she said. "We're going home."

SUNDAY MORNINGS were dicey. Alex never knew whether his mother would be in the mood for church or not—could go either way. If she was in the mood, there was no telling which church it would be. She had dragged him to First Presbyterian, St. Mark's Lutheran, the Unitarians, the Friends Meeting House and the Karma Chakra Buddhist Temple. They had even gone to some black Baptist church on South Pearl because, in his mother's words, "These people have turned their suffering to inspiration. You can learn from that." But he knew the real reason they had shown up that day. It was because the mayor of Albany was making a special appearance.

So the whole church-surfing thing was a fraud to the nth power, and Alex was sick of it. His objective was to stay in bed and feign sleep long enough to wear down her resolve. Let her go without him, especially after the aborted sneaker purchase.

It wasn't even the shoes so much, but the situation at the mall had put him into a funk. In just eleven days, the school year would be over, and he'd be turning sixteen facing another summer of doldrums. His true desire was to track down his long-absent father and get to know the man away from the tarnished lens of his mother. But Alex couldn't fathom making it all the way down to Fort Lauderdale on his own with no money and no driver's license.

"Alex," his mother said from the hall. "Time to get up."

He didn't budge. The door swung open. Let the game begin.

"I know you're awake," she continued. "Now get up."

His mother wasn't easily fooled. Her advantage was unpredictability. "I thought we'd go to the Friends Meeting House. It'll give you time to meditate on what you did last night."

To simulate REM, he shifted his eyeballs around in their sockets.

"It's after nine, come on." She gave him a soft nudge. "We've got thirty minutes."

He inhaled deeply.

"Alex, let's go!" She clapped her hands no more than six inches above his ear. Then she pushed him a little harder. "I know you're faking, now get yourself up." She flipped on the ceiling light and pulled the covers down to his waistline.

He felt a chilled rush. "You won't win this one," she said. The ability to sleep through such an onslaught was highly improbable. He anticipated her next move.

She laid a hand on his forehead and pried open an eyelid.

"Jesus Christ, mom!" He pushed her arm out of the way. "I'm not going to that zombie church."

"You'll go if I say so."

"No, actually, I won't. You can't make me."

"As long as you're living under my roof, you'll abide by my rules.

"It's barely even your house," Alex said. "Dad pays most of the mortgage." He pulled the covers over his head. "I should go live with him."

That silenced her for a moment. But then she recovered. "If I thought that was a good idea, I'd let you."

He didn't respond. If he pushed, she'd open a spigot of hostility. She'd call his father a loser or a flake (her favorite term), and she'd charge into a tirade on the importance of responsible parenting. It was too early in the morning to deal with that. Still, he had to say something. He lowered the covers enough to see the angst on her face. "You were the one who pushed him away."

She shook her head. "No, Alex, he did that all on his own."

That's when the phone rang. His mother wasn't the type to let a call go unanswered. At the very least, she'd check the caller ID. She was gone by the second ring.

His door remained open. He could hear her talking professional jargon with someone named Rebecca.

Hallelujah, church be damned.

CHAPTER TWO

It was Alex's favorite restaurant, no question—he loved the Thunderbird Grille. Even as his mother parked the Lexus, he could envision the meal before him: bacon and Swiss cheeseburger, sweet potato fries and a side of onion rings stacked up like a Christmas tree. To drink, he'd have Dr. Pepper. No reason to look at the menu. Instead, he'd scan the crowded restaurant for breasts—the bigger the better.

"What's the occasion?" he asked his mother as the hostess led them to a window-side booth. He knew there had to be some ulterior reason for this pleasant surprise. If it were solely up to her, they'd be dining at some French restaurant where they jazz everything up with sprigs and twigs.

"Your birthday's coming," she said.

"Yeah, but not for ten more days."

"We'll call it a pre-birthday surprise. Sixteen's a big one."

A smiling brunette, probably no older than twenty, arrived to take their order. Her shirt was partially unbuttoned but didn't reveal anything spectacular. Alex gave his order.

"Thanks," the waitress said, turning to his mother. "And for you?"

His mother ordered an Asian sesame chicken salad and a glass of pinot something-or-other. She closed her menu then added, "Oh, and a glass of iced water with a lime twist." Her face bore the weight of excess makeup, and her blond hair looked as if it was injected with vinyl. Not that Alex was any stellar prize. He was tall enough, nearly six feet, and his thick brown hair always generated a compliment from his hair stylist. *If I had hair like yours*, she invariably gushed. But, in a word, he was scrawny—all bones and angles. And if his smooth face was desirable to the opposite sex, he wouldn't have known, because it looked too much like the face of his mother.

His eyes lowered to the waitress's tight black pants and shapely butt as she gathered the menus and walked away. He looked back at his mother. "So this is for my birthday?"

"That's right." She unfolded her napkin and placed it on her lap. "I also wanted to discuss something with you."

"Oh no," he said. "Here we go."

"It's not bad. It's a good thing, really. Put your napkin on your lap."

He looked out the window at a little boy and his father holding hands as they cut across the parking lot. "Go ahead, say what you want to say." His napkin remained on the table.

"Well, as you know, I'm on the board of directors for several charitable organizations. One of these is Elder Spring. I'm sure I've told you about it."

"Don't think so."

"It's a very important cause—one that could really make a difference in society, especially in the lives of our senior citizens."

"Yeah, so?"

"This program matches a single elderly person with a qualifying family." She brought her hands together. "It has the makings of a revolutionary trend."

The waitress arrived with their beverages.

"Thank you," his mother said without looking up.

"Thanks," Alex said, glancing back at the waitress's shirt to see if she'd gotten any bigger since he placed his order.

His mother sipped her wine and did a kind of puckering thing with her lips. Then she gave a sideways smile indicating that the wine was marginally acceptable. "This program serves a real need for society. Think about it. There's a vast number of people who aren't well enough to live on their own, but they don't need or want the services of a nursing home." He could hear the timbre rising in her voice. She was onto one of her political kicks. Barring catastrophe, there'd be no stopping her until she had thoroughly exhausted the topic. He unwrapped his straw and slurped a third of his soda. Thank God for free refills, yet another reason he loved this place. His mother kept talking. "I received a call from my friend, Rebecca, who also sits on the board. She informed me that there's a candidate, a brilliant man who comes from down South."

"Okay, mom, what does all this have to do with us?"

"Please, Alex, let me finish. So this man—Lester Bray is his name—has agreed to come live with us on a trial basis."

Alex felt the air sucking out of his ribcage. "Wo, wo!" He held up a hand like a stop sign. "You gotta be kidding."

"This could be good for us," she said. "And for him."

"You're totally nuts," Alex said.

"I'm trying to do something positive for the family."

"How's bringing in some old fart gonna be good for our family?"

"He's not what you think. He's a bright African American man, a retired mechanical engineer from GE—"

"A black man," Alex said. "That's why you're doing this. You want to look good in the eyes of all your peacenik friends."

Despite the outer casing of makeup, her cheeks erupted into a pinkish red. "I will not have a racist living under my roof," she said. "That's not how I raised you."

"Fine, I'll move out. You and the old man can have the whole place to yourselves." It was the second time in one day that he'd threatened to leave home. Life couldn't be better.

The waitress arrived balancing a tray full of food. She placed the burger in front of Alex, the salad in front of his mother and the onion rings in the space between them. His mother, who looked poised for a tearful meltdown, slid out of the booth and briskly marched toward the bathroom. "Is she okay?" the waitress asked.

"Probably not," he said. "But it's not your fault."

"I'll bring you another Dr. Pepper."

"Thanks, that'd be great." Suddenly he felt that under the right circumstances he could fall in love with this girl, even if her breasts weren't that big. She had a sweet personality, he could tell.

He decided that his mother truly had gone nuts. Adopting an old man was almost beyond comprehension. He would have to find a way to reel her back onto solid ground. The best strategy was to give her another respectable cause to gnaw at.

He was well into his burger and stack of rings when she returned and slid to the center of the booth. She spread her napkin across her lap and drank the last of her wine. "What about a homeless shelter?" he asked. "There's plenty of black people there, no offense. You could bring them fancy meals and teach them the benefits of tofu and healthy living."

"I will not stand for you patronizing me! You think you've grown up. Well, you haven't! Not by a long shot."

"What's that supposed to mean?"

His mother waved in the direction of the waitress and held up her empty glass. Looking back at him, she said, "Part of growing up, Alex, is to set a good example. That's what we'll be doing with Mr. Bray."

Example for your résumé, he wanted to say. But his mouth was filled with scrumptious bacon cheeseburger. "Bullshit," was all he managed.

THE WEEK between his mother's big announcement and the arrival of Lester Bray passed without a word from Alex. Not that this was much of an achievement. He was an only child with a single mother. Silence was a way of life. He filled his time studying for finals or sketching—the one skill he knew he was good at, going all the way back to first grade. The ironic thing was that whenever someone came along and praised his work, he always screwed up, and not on purpose. It felt as if he was drawing exclusively for them and no longer from his own imagination. So he liked to draw alone, and he liked to draw whatever his brain conjured up at the moment.

But that wasn't exactly true, because even though his mind was now riddled with images of old black men, he refused to put his imagined Mr. Bray to paper. He could hardly fathom the idea that such a being was actually coming to live in the room next to his. Worse— they'd be sharing the same bathroom.

The day had come. He peered out his second-story bedroom window and stared at a white van below. Its side door slid open, and out popped a woman. Not just any woman, but a brown-haired beauty, tall and dreamily proportioned, with a toothpaste commercial smile. He knew from his mother's nonstop chatter that this was Rebecca, Mr. Bray's caseworker. Alex couldn't stop staring as she guided the old man safely from van to driveway. That's when his mother bounded out of the house and shook everyone's hand, including the driver of the van. The driver remained outside, smoking a cigarette, while Rebecca lugged a suitcase behind Lester and Alex's mother.

A good son, Alex knew, would have charged down the stairs, introduced himself and smiled graciously as the pleasantries volleyed back and forth. That same good son would've offered refreshments and carried up the old man's bag. But Alex couldn't get himself to budge. His mother was in charge, as she had been all week. Throughout his vigil of silence, she had made phone call after phone call. She told the moving people when to come and where to put Lester's stuff, including an old Cadillac Deville, which apparently wasn't classy enough to park on their driveway. Instead, the ancient beast sat curbside, looking totally out of place. She had called the various doctors in charge of Mr. Bray's care, and she'd created a list—a Post-It Note from Hell—of all the maladies he was diagnosed with. There was diabetes, enlarged heart, hypertension, angina, emphysema and osteoarthritis. Amazing the old man was still upright and breathing.

Alex knew he should have felt sympathetic. But what he felt was that this whole thing—this sick old man and Alex's freight train of a mother—pushed him right out of the picture. He put his headphones on, but decided to keep the music off. He approached the staircase, out of everyone's line of vision, and listened while his mother gave a guided tour of their house. She began in the living room, saying, "This room doesn't get used as much as I'd like. We spend most of our time in the kitchen and great room."

"I like the color," Lester said. His words came out sharp and surprisingly vibrant for a man riddled with disease.

"I'm so glad you do," his mother said. "It's called Caramel Macchiato from the Starbuck's collection at Sherwin Williams. I think it's a hit." Pure crap, Alex thought. The color was a shade browner than lint from the dryer.

"That's such a lovely bay window," Rebecca said. "Shame not to use this room more often."

"I know, but that's our life. We're very casual." It was the kind of nauseating response that made Alex wish he'd been switched at birth.

The three of them advanced to the kitchen, just below the staircase. As if anyone cared, his mother proclaimed that the walls were painted Evergreen Mist. She tried to downplay the cabinets, which were glazed and stained to look like mahogany but were actually maple. Then she added that the countertops were buckwheat granite. It was a painful conversation and it would have gotten worse. She would've gone on blabbering about the espresso-stained dining room table under the brushed nickel chandelier, maybe even the leather sectional in the den. But, mercifully, the old man interrupted. "Heard you've got a son."

"Yes, his name's Alex. Would you like to meet him now, or should I continue with the tour?"

"Better make it now. I'm pretty rundown, could use a rest."

"That's perfectly understandable," she said, "my goodness, after all you've been through."

Alex darted back into his room. He closed the door silently, slid into bed and began searching for a song on his iPod that would best typify the moment. If there was one entitled *The Promise of Embarrassment*, he would have selected it. But he went through two compromise songs, barely listening, before his mother finally knocked.

"Alex," she said, "there are people I want you to meet."

He didn't respond. To do so would have negated an entire week of silence.

She opened the door and walked in. "Take the headphones off, please." She poked her head back into the hall. "Mr. Bray, Rebecca, you can come in."

Lester entered breathing like an old steam engine. Stairs must have maxed out his already compromised lungs. He nodded. Rebecca was still out in the hall.

Alex nodded back while his mother grabbed his headphones.

"Give me that back!" His first words to his mother in nearly eight days.

"Don't be rude," she said. "Say hello to Mr. Bray."

"Hello," Alex said.

Lester said, "Hey, kid," then added, "nice room." He scratched a section of scalp above his ear. What little hair he had was blizzard white. There were dark splotches on his already dark face. It was the kind of face that was probably ugly even before it got old. The old man's eyes scanned the room settling on the sketches above Alex's headboard. The largest featured a trail under the jagged ridge of an escarpment, sprays of water coming down on would-be hikers. Another was a cutaway of a motorcycle engine with cam, valve, spring, piston and crankshaft. There were a few trees Alex liked and a couple of hybrid animals, part reptile-part human. And even though Alex had sketched hundreds of partially undressed women, there were only five worthy enough to put on display.

Lester's eyes shifted to the wall at the long side of the bed. Centered above was a Rand McNally street map of Fort Lauderdale and a green pin midway down the stretch of coast, on the beach side of Route A1A. "Interesting," he said but didn't press. And Alex certainly wasn't going to explain the meaning of the map.

"Rebecca," Alex's mother said, "you can come in."

Lester stepped aside to make room for Rebecca. She entered, wearing the same inviting smile from the driveway. "Hi, Alex," she said, waving her hand.

Alex tried to appear relaxed and confident, but when he said her name it came out with a slight chirp. He could feel the heat coming off his face.

Lester chuckled. "Wouldn't you know? She sure got his attention."

CHAPTER THREE

Alex sat in the back row of Mr. Myer's seventh period Geometry class. It was the final exam, collectively known as the Myer Mystifier. But Alex would utilize a time-tested strategy, and no one could accuse him of cheating. He had discovered the tool at age ten when he won a four-way bike race. Part of the credit should have gone to his father, because during the entire race Alex imagined that his eyes were not exclusively his. His pumping legs were not just his own legs, and the hands shifting the gears were more than the hands of a ten-year-old. His body had shared all bike-related maneuvers with his father. And when Alex cruised to victory, he sensed his father watching with pride.

He called it the Father Mind Game, and it grew to become an important part of his life. It was infinitely flexible, because when you didn't know someone you could pretty much make up the whole scenario. You didn't have to deal with the realities of the actual person. So one moment his imaginary father could be a master artist, guiding him while he sketched a beautiful woman. Or, in this case, his father was a mathematical wiz tackling one geometric quandary after another. And then tomorrow, while sitting for the driver's license permit test, his father would transform into Rules of the Road Expert, as per New York State.

With twenty-two minutes to spare, he closed his test booklet and set down his pencil, nodding a little fatherly thank you. He could get up, grab a yearbook from the stack and be on his way home. But he would wait. He would not be singled out as the antisocial brainiac people took him for. Plus he wanted to get Britney Garrand to sign his yearbook. That would give him something to dream about all summer long.

"Ten minutes," Mr. Myer announced as he paced up and down the aisles scanning for last-minute cheaters.

Alex sunk his face into his hands and closed his eyes. In addition to this being the last day of tenth grade, it was also his birthday. Later, at home, he would open a few presents. They would be obvious things he'd asked for weeks earlier. No surprises.

Like every birthday, he hoped for something from his father. He pictured a hefty box wrapped in brown paper, postmarked Florida. There'd be a letter inside the box explaining why, after all these years, the man never wrote, never called. It had to be something good. Son, I'm a spy with the Federal Government. Or perhaps his father was part of the witness protection program. If he called, he'd be risking his and Alex's life.

But those scenarios no longer fit because Alex had Googled the name Scott Riley and found that, despite all his imagined personas, the man was actually head chef and owner of some posh Fort Lauderdale restaurant. Which was what his mother had told him anyway. A little more research and Alex discovered his father's home address, which created a new sense of urgency. At first, he requested, and later he begged his mother to take him down there. Her pre-packaged refusals filled him with hatred.

Deeper inside his father's package would be a variety of items — nothing new and nothing made in China. Each would have special meaning. Like an engraved pocket watch handed down from an unknown grandfather. A faded baseball cap with the name of some faraway college his father had attended. A retro CD of the music he had listened to. And, best of all, a recording of his father's voice telling of his regrets.

Alex cursed himself for indulging in such fantasy. It never worked out. There would be no package at the front door. Not this year, not ever.

The final bell yanked him back to reality. "Pencils down," Mr. Myer said. "Turn in your tests. If you've paid for a yearbook, your name will be on this list. Stealing yearbooks is not an option."

About half the class, including Alex, got up and clustered around the teacher's desk. The remaining students poured over their booklets, feverishly rifling through pages, scrutinizing theorems and axioms. Some were sweating.

Alex fed his booklet through an opening between classmates, checked off his name among the paid customers and picked up a yearbook. He wedged it under his arm. There wasn't much time. Britney would be getting out of American History on the other side of Sloan Hall, two buildings away. He slung his backpack over his shoulder and jostled himself through the packed hallway.

Outside, he quickened his pace just shy of an actual run. He never ran. It was part of his philosophy. Running meant some sort of urgency, that you didn't have your shit together. Above all, Alex had his shit together. That's what he needed people to think.

His pace turned casual as he cornered the eastern face of Sloan Hall. A straight line of maple trees umbrellaed two rows of picnic tables, and every table was surrounded by students. All of Delmar High, it seemed, was outside in front of Sloan Hall. People were chattering and laughing and gawking at the coffee-table-size book. It was the year's culmination—the moment when a friend would summon his wits and verbal command and try to say something perfect for the other friend. Or, most often, he'd spew away with phony sentiment.

Five tables down. There she stood, surrounded by a dozen other students. Britney Garrand wasn't the hottest girl on campus. Her nose, for one, was pointy. And she still wore braces. But he could appreciate her deeper beauty. The risk was that he would be caught staring at her. Her opinion of him would be marred forever. His insides were pounding. He had to do something. The best strategy was to find another person to hang out with while the crowd around Britney thinned.

There was one classmate nearby whom Alex could theoretically call a friend, though that was stretching the term by a mile. It was Jimmy Reece—one of the fattest and definitely the smelliest kid in tenth grade. Jimmy was leaning against a tree, flipping haphazardly through pages of his yearbook.

Alex made his approach while keeping Britney and the crowd around her in his peripheral vision. "Hey Jimmy, what's up?"

"Yo, Alex," Jimmy said. He closed his yearbook. "This thing bites."

Alex looked at the cover of his book. "I'm sure it does." There was a beaver, the school's mascot, against a backdrop of psychedelic swirls of orange and blue. Scattered along the colorful ribbons were dozens of faces of students and teachers. Someone had tried pretty hard to be artistic, Alex thought, but to share such an observation with Jimmy was to use sign language with a blind man.

Jimmy squinted at his book. He needed glasses but was probably too poor or too lazy to get them. "Hey, that's Coach Piper," he said then laughed stupidly.

To avoid a shot of Jimmy's breath, Alex backed away. He saw that there were only four people standing around Britney. Just a couple of minutes, he figured. He flipped open his book and looked at Jimmy. "Wanna sign?"

Jimmy gave off a kind of sinister grin. "I don't normally, but in your case, no problemo. Here, you can sign mine too."

They exchanged yearbooks. Jimmy's was sticky. Alex flipped to the first blank page. He looked up and saw that she was starting to move. He wrote, *Have a great summer*, scribbled his name and gave the book back to Jimmy.

Alex returned his yearbook under his arm, "I gotta go."

"Yo, on the upside," Jimmy said, producing the same demonic grin. It was made worse by all that stinking flesh surrounding it.

Alex nearly broke his rule about running as he tried to catch up to Britney. He had to reach her before she landed herself into another clique, and then he'd be left standing off to the side again like some crazed predator. He made a cone of his hand and yelled, "Britney!"

She stopped and turned. Her face appeared to be straining—either from sun glare or failure to recall his name.

He was gracious enough to let her off the hook. "It's Alex," he said, "from Anthropology."

"Of course," she said with reduced strain. "You drew that ape on the board with horns. Pretty cool."

Not one of his better drawings, but at least she remembered him. A pitiful thought remained. She might not have known his name. He certainly didn't want to wrestle with that prospect all summer long. So before asking her to sign his yearbook, he decided to test her. He cleared his throat and asked, "You remember my last name?"

She gave a little smirk then said, "Huh...I believe it rhymes with *smiley.*"

If her intention was to make him smile, it worked, like she'd gone up to him with her fingers and broadened his lips. Once he regained the capacity to speak, he said, "I was thinking maybe you'd sign my yearbook."

"Sure," she said. "And you can sign mine."

He opened Britney's book and was stunned by the abundance of entries. Page after page was filled with sweetness. Her American History teacher, Miss Caruso, wrote half a page of pure tripe. There were hearts and smiley faces and even two pictures of turtles. What was that all about?

He flipped to a blank corner and thought about what to write. He shot down about five things as being too desperate, too horny, too cryptic or just plain scary. She was already done and waiting. He was forced to go with vanilla basic. *Britney,* he wrote. *You seem like a wonderful person. I hope in junior year I'll get to know you better. Alex.* He closed the book and raised it toward her.

She was holding his yearbook between her thumb and forefinger, like the way you'd hold a dead rat by its tail. He thought of Jimmy. Fat bastard must've gotten his sticky ooze all over the thing.

She returned his book and said, "Maybe you should be a little choosier about who you let sign this."

"Why's that?"

She smiled brightly. Then she said, "Have a great summer, Alex."

"You too," he said. His heart was soaring. The moment was pure electricity. He watched her walk about twenty steps before being engulfed, once again, by classmates.

He flipped open his book and found the page. In neat cursive, it read: *Dear Alex RILEY, I disagree. Britney,* followed by a little smiley face.

Just above was Jimmy's handwriting.

You're a fucking loser—JR

CHAPTER FOUR

He opened the front door and slammed his yearbook on the faux marble floor then slammed the door behind him. He marched past the book and into the kitchen, wondering if he'd startled the old man, but not really caring if he did. He put three hot dogs on a glass plate and nuked them while retrieving a soda from the fridge. Then he brought the meal upstairs and tried to make it past Lester's room undetected.

The old man came out of the bathroom, nearly colliding with the plate.

"Hey," Alex said without looking up.

"Hey kid," Lester said. "Heard today's your birthday."

"That's right."

"Well, happy birthday then."

Alex raised his chin slightly. "Thanks."

Lester pointed down the hall and said, "I like your drawings. You've got a natural talent."

"Thanks."

"But I was wondering," Lester said, now staring at Alex's door. "What's the deal with the map?"

"It's nothing," Alex said.

"You telling me you got a map of Fort Lauderdale on your wall for no good reason?"

"Yeah, so?"

"You're a liar, kid, and not a very good one."

"Why do you want to know?" This had to be the worst birthday on record. "You've been there?"

"I have," Lester said. "I'm from the South. One thing about Southerners: we drive, and I mean all over the place."

Alex raised his eyes to a conversational level. "When were you last there?"

"I don't know, maybe thirty years. Place is probably unrecognizable from when I last saw it."

Alex was searching for something to say, but found nothing.

"Listen, kid." The old man checked to make sure his fly was zipped. "You don't need to tell me anything. Just learn to be a better liar. In this world, you've got to be believable. That's the least of it."

"I'll work on that," Alex said.

"Then again, I'm an old goat. Half of what I say is garbage."

In the midst of his misery, Alex couldn't help but smile, if only for a second.

"Eat your dogs before they get cold."

IT TOOK about forty seconds to eat three hot dogs. He washed them down with soda and belched loud enough to vibrate the floorboards. Then he flopped himself onto his bed and put on his headphones, soon realizing there was nothing he wanted to listen to. He turned down the volume, closed his eyes and thought of how pathetic his life had become. Sixteen would be more of the same.

He could hear the old man moving things around in his bedroom groaning all the while. There was a loud thud and a jingling of metal, followed by cursing. Something fell, hopefully not the old man.

Alex darted over to Lester's room and saw the old man crouched on the floor, picking up coins. The drawers to his dresser were laid out on his bed. Alex knocked on the open door and said, "What happened?"

Lester looked up. "Goddamn jar of change fell when I tried to move this dresser."

"Why do you want to move it?" The thing was pretty well centered against the back wall. To the left was a window and a burgundy recliner, to the right stood a wicker hamper.

"Some idiot put the thing too close to my chair," Lester said. "It's too cramped when I sit."

"That idiot would be my mother."

Lester said, "Hmm," then scooped up some more coins.

"I can help if you want."

"Hope you're not a thief."

Alex got down on his knees. "If I was, I'd pick something better than your pocket change." The pristine Cadillac would have been his choice or maybe the old man's laptop. Beyond these, there didn't seem to be anything Lester had of value.

"You don't think this is much. Add it up and I'll bet there's two hundred bucks if there's a dime."

"Why don't you get it exchanged? They've got machines, you know."

"I would, kid, but the problem is I can't carry the son of a bitch anymore. Maybe I could get your help, give you a cut."

Alex nodded and raked up a cluster of coins. "Don't worry about it. On the house."

Lester pointed a crooked finger toward the dresser. "I want it two feet that way." His hand was a gnarly mess, like something Picasso would've sketched then probably sold for a fortune.

"No problem," Alex said. He got up and started pushing the dresser across the wall-to-wall carpet. It was light without the drawers. He stopped and looked down at Lester.

"A little more."

Alex gave another push.

"That's good, kid. Thanks."

"You want the drawers back in?"

Lester looked up and said, "What do you think?"

Alex smiled. "Yeah, that was pretty stupid."

The route between bed and dresser was blocked by Lester and an array of coins still scattered about the floor. Alex helped gather them up and then helped Lester to his chair. The old man was breathing pretty heavily, and from what? He hadn't moved more than ten feet. Alex picked up the jar of coins, set it on the dresser and began putting the drawers back in.

Lester's breathing slowed. "Thanks again, kid. You're not so bad after all."

Alex nodded and walked to the door. He paused, one foot in the room, one in the hall. He was studying Lester's face, how weather-beaten it looked. And his eyes. Alex had probably never looked into a black man's eyes before, at least not consciously. They were really black—not in a bad way, like *your soul is black*, but in a mysterious way. "The map," Alex finally said. "You were asking about the map."

Lester placed his hands on his lap and said, "Go on."

"Well, that's where my father lives, Fort Lauderdale."

"Figured it was something like that," Lester said. "He's pretty far away. Guess you don't see him much."

"Try never. Not since I was a year old."

Lester nodded slowly. "Well, that's a shame...a shame for both of you."

"It's no big deal," Alex said. "It's nothing."

Lester stopped nodding. "There you go again, lying."

Alex could hear the front door opening. "Alex!" his mother yelled. He didn't answer.

"Alex!" she yelled louder. "Get down here and pick up your book! It's blocking the door. You know better than that."

Lester waved a disfigured hand. "See ya, kid."

FOR BETTER or worse, Alex was back to speaking with his mother who had just come to the kitchen after visiting with Lester in his bedroom and inviting him down for the birthday celebration. Something seemed to be bothering her. She was standing at the sink, cleaning lettuce like she was trying to pulverize it.

"What did he say?" Alex wanted to know.

"Oh, he'll be down," his mother said without looking away.

"Yeah, but what did he say?"

"Mr. Bray wants to drive his car. That's all. And the doctors say he shouldn't, at least not yet."

"And you're playing hardball with him?"

"Hush," she said. "He'll be down soon."

Alex set the table for four, and he moved his stack of presents and the three helium balloons to the far couch where they wouldn't be such a spectacle.

In a little while, Lester ambled his way to the dining room table and leaned against the back of the farthest chair from the kitchen. He appeared to be trying to catch his breath while staring at the ruby-colored placemats and matching cloth napkins. "Who's the fourth?" he asked.

Alex didn't want to answer. He looked over at his mother who had moved on to chopping veggies.

"Oh, that would be my boyfriend, Bill," she said. "He should be here any minute."

Alex poured glasses of water. "Horny bastard," he muttered.

"Alex, hush," his mother said. "There'll be none of that tonight."

"You don't like him?" Lester asked Alex.

"I call him Bill Blue Balls. He only comes over for one reason—"

"Alex!" his mother yelled. "Not another word."

Lester chuckled and lowered himself into the chair while Alex brought over the glasses of water.

"Sorry there's nothing from me," Lester said, motioning toward the couch. The old man's eyesight was sharp enough to make out the stack of presents on the other side of the unlit great room. It certainly wasn't poor vision that kept him from driving.

"No problem." Alex sat down to Lester's right. "I don't need anything."

The front door opened. "Hello everybody." It was Bill's jovial voice.

"Just in time," Alex's mother said. She dried off her hands and went out to the living room. The two exchanged a couple of kisses, and then she said, "Come meet Mr. Bray."

Bill walked in carrying a pizza box. He had a bag in each hand. One was greasy, probably wings. The other had a wrapped gift partially sticking out. He set the items on the counter and said, "Hello, Mr.

Bray, Bill Baler." He walked toward Lester. "I've heard great things about you."

"Same here," Lester said, shaking Bill's hand.

Alex's mother placed a wooden bowl with two wooden utensils at the center of the table. She said, "Salad first everybody" in a kind of playful way. But Alex knew she'd been burned by Lester about the driving. So beneath her playfulness, she was exerting her don't-mess-with-my-authority stance, which Alex knew all too well. He wondered how much of a pushover Lester might prove to be.

As she began doling out salad, Lester cleared his throat and said, "So, ma'am, what other rules do you have?"

She offered a tight smile.

"This ought to be good," Alex said.

"Well," she said, "there really aren't any."

Alex coughed out the word *bullshit*.

Bill pointed and said, "Be respectful, Alex."

"He lives here now," Alex said. "He should know mom's ground rules."

"There aren't any ground rules," his mother said. "Not for him."

"So you're not going to make him go to church?"

"No, but he can come along he'd like. We could even visit his church, if he'll have us."

Lester smiled. "No offense, ma'am, but I haven't seen the inside of a church in years. Never had any use for it. Way I see it, no minister or priest ever came back from the dead. They don't know any better than you or I about what's on the other side. It's all a bunch of man-made hocus-pocus."

Alex flipped an elbow toward his mother and said, "Take that!" Then he glanced at Lester, impressed.

"Well, Mr. Bray," she said, "that's what makes this country great. We're all entitled to our opinion."

"Yes we are," Lester said. "As long as your opinion doesn't encroach on my freedom."

"Slam," Alex said. "Score two for Mr. Bray." He looked at his mother who was now seated directly across, red cheeks glistening under the chandelier.

"Sorry," Lester said, "I get a little carried away." Then he looked at Alex with raised eyebrows as if to say, *You got your hands full with this broad.*

The conversation was pretty mellow while everyone ate pizza, but then Bill made the mistake of asking Lester who he liked in the upcoming primary.

Lester wiped his fingers with a napkin and took a sip of water. He put the glass down and said, "Don't care much for any of 'em."

Alex's mother jumped right in. "Have you looked at their platforms?"

"Platforms," Lester said, as if mocking the very idea. "Now there's a real good word, Mrs. Riley. You been around as long as I have, you'd know that every politician lies. Every one of them has his price. Today's platform is tomorrow's pimp list."

It started again. Her cheeks went Macintosh red.

Bill reached for her hand. "Honey, I'm sorry I brought it up."

"I'll bet you're sorry," Alex said. "Sorry you won't be getting any tonight."

"That's enough!" His mother pounded the butt end of her knife into her placemat. She gave Alex a fierce look. "You don't talk to him that way. Ever!"

"All right, mom, chill."

"And, Mr. Bray," she said. "I'd appreciate a bit more civility from you with regard to religion and politics. My son is quite impressionable. He's too young to turn into a cynic."

Lester put his napkin on his plate. "It's the only way I know, ma'am. I'm too old to change. You want me to leave, just say the word."

"I didn't mean that," she said. "I would just like...a little...civility." Her nose registered a sniffle. "That's all."

Lester turned to Alex. "Sorry I ruined your birthday, kid."

"You didn't," Alex said, thinking of Jimmy Reece, the fat bastard. "It was ruined before I left school."

CHAPTER FIVE

By far the single worst moment of the month was the fifteen minutes Alex had to spend with Dr. Kruger. It might not have been so bad if the shrink had stuck with his job description of simply checking out how the drugs were working. But the guy was an old school shrink, prying into Alex's business and then sharing those details with his mother. So he had to be careful, especially when it came to discussing the medications, which he was supposed to be taking everyday.

They turned north onto Delaware Avenue. "Maybe I should've asked you before I agreed to it," his mother said.

"Agreed to what?"

"Having Mr. Bray live with us. Maybe I should have cleared it with you first."

"When do you ever clear things with me?" Alex wore a red baseball cap. His body was slanted toward the door, face turned to the world outside the car. His mood was buffeted only by the fact that, after the shrink, Alex would get to take the driver's license permit exam. One more little notch toward independence. "Lester's here anyway. So that's that."

"Perhaps we should cancel the arrangement. Have Mr. Bray live in a more appropriate place. Those stairs, for one, are a real challenge for him. I can't imagine how horrifying it would be if he fell."

"That's your reason?" Alex said. "The stairs?"

"Well, yes, that's the main one."

"What if I said he should stay? You never gave me a vote before. My vote is he stays."

"You're just being oppositional."

"Well you're a flip-flopper." He turned and looked at her. "Two weeks ago you were saying how great it would be for our *family*. Now you want to kick him out on his ass."

"It's just not an appropriate place for him. If you thought about it, you'd agree. And I find his views a little," she gripped the steering wheel with both hands, "well...crude."

"He says what he means. What's wrong with that?"

They pulled up to the familiar gray office building with tinted windows that were permanently shut. Even though Alex had no idea what he wanted to do career-wise, he knew he never wanted to work in a place where you couldn't open the damn windows. Everything else was negotiable. Second nameplate down: Seth Kruger, MD, Psychiatry.

His mother went up to the receptionist and gave Alex's name while he grabbed a copy of *The New Yorker* and sat down. He started thumbing through the magazine, stopping only to check out the cartoons.

Dr. Kruger stuck his head through the doorway. "Alex, come on back."

He got up with the magazine and followed to the office. He sat in the overstuffed chair farthest away from the doctor's desk.

Kruger sat behind his desk. "So, Alex," he said, "how are you?" He opened the thickening file.

"Fine." Alex's baseball cap provided a barricade against eye contact. His index finger held his place in the magazine. He flipped it open.

"I'd like you to put that aside."

"Why? You get paid either way." He looked at a joke with two cats sitting at a dining room table. What was it about intellectuals and cat humor?

"I'm here to help you," Dr. Kruger said, "not waste your time." He scribbled something in the chart.

"Help me with what?"

"Well, to make better choices, for one, and to help you develop positive social connections. Those are my priorities."

"I'm fine. I don't need any of your help."

"Let's face it; we could all use a little guidance these days." He leaned back, clasping his hands below his bearded chin. "How are the medications working?"

There were three of them: Concerta for attention deficit disorder, Zyprexa for oppositional defiant disorder and Lexapro for depression. Despite the sexy names, all three were total crap. Alex had started flushing them ten months ago, when his mother took the bold step of putting him in charge of their disbursement. "Fine," he said, "no problems."

"How's your sleep?"

"Fine, no problem."

"Your appetite?"

"Fine, no problem."

"How about your focus on schoolwork?"

"Fine, no problem. School's out."

"How'd you do?" Kruger asked. "How were your grades?"

"Fine."

"I can check with your mother."

"Fine, go check." He found another joke featuring a parrot in a cage next to a busty old lady.

"How about your friends? Have you made any new friends?"

"I've got plenty." True answer: zero. "Thanks for your concern." His thoughts shifted to Jimmy Reece and the violence he would love to wreak on that bloated, stinking excuse for a human being.

"Too much isolation is a dangerous thing."

"No reason to worry, doc." Alex finished the magazine but kept it on his lap in case things got really intolerable. His restless eyes scanned the array of books shelved behind the doctor. These were meant solely for show, Alex figured, because there was one book he had inverted nearly a year ago, flipping it in the brief moment Kruger left him alone in the office to talk privately with his mother. It was a beefy textbook entitled *Psychopathology of Childhood and Adolescence*, and it was still upside-down staring at him.

Then Dr. Kruger did something unexpected. He reached down below his desk and pulled out a newspaper. The front page featured a photo of a playground. In the center a girl was crying, hugging a woman. The headline said that two were dead and seven injured in a Dallas school shooting. "Do you know about this story?" Kruger asked, pointing to the body of text.

"Nope."

"Won't be as much press coverage as Virginia Tech or Columbine, but that doesn't lessen the pain felt by these families." He shook his head as if personally affected. "To me, as a family man, this is the worst thing imaginable."

"What's your point?"

The doctor kicked back in his chair and placed his hands together, professor style. "In some ways the shooters are always the same. They're always male, always loners and always filled with rage. They've been bullied in school. And if there's a father in the house, he's either too busy or too out of touch to make a positive impact."

"Sounds like you've got the case pretty well nailed," Alex said. "You should write a letter to the editor."

"And smart too," Kruger added, now staring at Alex. "These killers are smart enough to go undetected by their teachers, their parents." He intensified his tone. "Maybe even their psychiatrists."

Alex looked once more at the picture. There was a figure he hadn't noticed initially. It was a cop standing in the background, crew-cut and a menacing stare. That stare seemed to accuse the photographer of the worst kind of exploitation. But now, mixed with Kruger's words, the cop's stare made Alex feel like the accused one.

"I think you know what I'm getting at." Kruger folded the paper. "You fit the profile...and it concerns me deeply."

Alex remained silent. His chest was pounding.

"I've been thinking about increasing the Zyprexa," Kruger said. "Just enough to give you a little more behavioral control. The current dose may not be enough."

Alex tried to shake off the implications of being a mass murderer. "Do what you gotta do, doc!" He stood up, tossed the magazine aside and marched out of the office. He walked past the reception desk, past his mother. He went outside and sat on the trunk of the Lexus, trying to rid himself of the doctor's words.

His mother got in the car and put on her sunglasses without saying anything. They passed a hodgepodge of specialty shops, restaurants, a gas station and a few houses that hadn't yet caved to commercial development. "I want him gone," Alex said.

"Sad as it is," his mother responded, "that's one thing we agree on."

"Really? That's a first."

"I thought we'd give it a few more weeks," she said. "But that'll just make it harder on everyone."

"Wait, mom, who are you talking about?"

"Mr. Bray, of course."

"Bullshit—I was talking about Kruger. I don't want Mr. Bray to leave. He should stay. But I can't stand that asshole shrink anymore."

"Watch your language," she said. She was all reflexes when it came to profanity. "You and I can discuss a gradual tapering." She made a descending staircase with her non-driving hand. "When you're ready."

"It's been three years, mom. Three years of babbling bullshit! I don't wanna see that dick-face again."

"Enough!" She sped the car around a right-turning Mercedes. "We might be able to come up with something...as long as your behavior doesn't degenerate."

"What something?" he asked.

"If we can get the pediatrician to continue your medications, we could probably stop seeing Dr. Kruger."

"Perfect," he said. "I'm in."

"That's only part of it. The other part—and I regret having to say this—is that Mr. Bray must take residence elsewhere."

"You're serious. I can't believe it. You'd use the shrink to get rid of Lester."

"That's not how I would put it."

"But that's how it is."

"You've got your interpretation, I've got mine. I'm only trying to do what's right—"

"Don't say, for our family, please. I've heard enough bullshit for one day."

The deal she proposed was shameful. He knew that much. But the shame was mixed with an emerging freedom. No more shrink. How liberating was that?

He crouched down in his seat and pulled his cap a little lower. "Okay," he said, "I'll go along."

CHAPTER SIX

In an ideal reality, Lester would have been zapped into someone else's home right after Alex had agreed to the deal. Everything back to normal at the Riley household. But when Alex came downstairs for breakfast, Lester was hunkered in, eating a bowl of Special K and reading the *Times Union*.

"Morning," Alex said, unable to make eye contact.

"Good morning, kid."

Alex prepared a bowl of cereal and sat at the opposite end of the table. His guilt had kept him up most of the night, and he was tired. He yawned audibly without covering his mouth.

Lester looked up from the paper, eyeballs hovering over a pair of reading glasses. "What the hell you got in there?"

"What?"

"In your mouth?" Lester pointed a finger.

"It's a tongue piercing," Alex said.

"It's plain stupid is what it is." The old man flipped to the obituaries. "I'll never know why you kids do that sort of thing. But I guess you got your reasons."

It was the last thing Alex wanted to talk about. He finished his cereal, got up and poured himself a second bowl.

"I was thinking," Lester said without looking up from the paper, "you got a good idea."

"About what?"

"Getting my change turned to cash. If you got the time, we could do it today."

Alex couldn't think of a handy excuse, so he said, "No problem."

But there was a problem, actually two. The first was that Lester wasn't supposed to drive, and Alex had only just gotten his permit. He'd never actually driven a motorized vehicle unless you want to count go-carts at the FunPlex. Then there was his mother, away at work in her cushy office, leaving Alex clueless as to when she'd pull the plug on Lester. Of all the things to be pissed at her for, this one took the prize.

He now realized that he'd given in too easily. If she'd wanted Lester gone badly enough, she would have made more concessions...perhaps even in a trip to Fort Lauderdale.

An hour after breakfast, they were sitting in Lester's Cadillac ready to make their way to the Price Chopper grocery store. "Let's see if she turns," the old man said. He put the key in the ignition and pumped the gas. The engine sputtered then smoothed itself out to a steady rhythm. He pulled the transmission lever into drive.

"Nice car," Alex said. "You get it new?"

"Course I did." He adjusted the rearview mirror. "Took ownership of this beauty well before you were born."

They galloped forward and quickly reached a decent cruising speed. Alex pointed, "Take a left. It's about three miles."

The car had a musty, leathery smell, but it wasn't unpleasant. It was all black, inside and out, making the silver knobs and the white speedometer numbers stand out like lines on the road. "Feels good to drive again," Lester said. "If it were up to me, I'd be laid to rest on the day I have to give up my keys." He pushed the accelerator.

Alex could feel the instantaneous suck of fuel and the thrust of the big V-8. Healthy sounding engine, and strong. The old man had definitely babied it. They drove for a mile or so before anyone spoke.

Then Alex asked, "Where'd you live before?"

"Hospital," Lester said. "But I don't remember much of that. Three days I was in a diabetic coma. Then I woke up. All I could see was this fat white man in the bed next to me, snoring his ass off."

Alex smiled at the mental image.

"I made a slow recovery, apparently too slow for my landlord. He showed up at the hospital to evict me. I was renting some god-awful apartment in Schenectady for a couple of years. Before that, I had a pretty big house. Not like yours, but it was nice."

"Why'd you move out?"

"My damn sister talked me into selling." He paused to catch his breath. "I broke my hip mowing the lawn. House was on a pretty steep hill, you see, and I fell right next to that running lawnmower. Scared the crap out of me...literally."

"You mean you actually shit your pants?"

"I did," Lester said. "And that's not the only time. Getting old sucks."

Alex laughed nervously. "So you came right from the hospital to live with us?"

"Oh, they wanted to put me in a nursing home. But I told them they'd have to shoot me first. No way was I was going into one of them hell-holes alive." He made an ugly grimace. "That's when I met Rebecca. I call her Dixie Cup 'cause she's from Georgia." The ugly face was gone. "That girl could've talked me into government bonds."

He pulled the car into a handicapped spot, reached for the glove box and pulled out a blue tag with a stick figure in a wheelchair. "This right here's about the only good thing about getting old."

Alex placed the big jar in a shopping cart and wheeled it to the store while Lester trailed behind. By the time the old man arrived, Alex was already scooping coins into the machine, which kept a running tally minus its eight-percent cut, all the while spitting out the occasional Canadians. When it was done, the little screen read $263.24. Alex pressed a button for the receipt.

"Told you," Lester said, "more money than you thought." He brought the receipt over to customer service. Then he counted out the cash and put all but a twenty into his wallet. "Here you go, kid, take this."

"Thanks, but no," Alex said, sliding his hands into his pockets.

"Don't be stubborn."

Alex didn't want to make a scene, so he took it. But back in the car he returned the handicapped tag in the glove box and slid the twenty underneath.

"I saw that," Lester said. "Put it in your pocket. You should get a cut."

"I don't want it," Alex said, shutting the compartment.

"Well, suit yourself. Can't say I've got much use for it either. Damn sure ain't going to get my tongue pierced." He backed out of the spot and turned away from the plaza. "Why'd you get that done anyway?"

"Piss off my mother," Alex said.

Lester chuckled and slapped the steering wheel. "Guess that's not such a bad reason. You'll grow out of it, though. I had the same feeling about my mother for a time. She was as bad as a drill sergeant— should've been a drill sergeant."

"Mine too."

"But when she passed, nearly twenty years ago, I really did miss her. She died in the same house where I grew up, in Terrell, Alabama. I made her funeral, but I haven't been home since."

Even though the temperature inside the car had to be ninety degrees, Alex's guilt made him feel cold. After a couple of miles, he asked, "Ever think of going back?"

"My sister's the only one left—lives in that same ramshackle house." He slowed the Cadillac and turned onto the dead-end street. "I've been telling her for years I'd make a visit. But it always seemed like too much trouble."

"Your driving's good," Alex said. "You could do it."

"Kid, in case you haven't noticed, I'm an old goat. Ain't much drive left in me." He parked on the street and killed the engine. Then he patted the dashboard. "Plenty left in this Caddy, though."

THE LATE afternoon sun shot across Alex's room from the open window. He was sitting on his bed with his sketchpad, but he sprang to his feet when he heard a car pulling up to the house. It was a bright red Scion with an open sunroof. Rebecca stepped out and smiled her way to the front porch, because Lester was sitting there playing solitaire. He was an oddball. Even though the porch was no bigger than a broom closet, and hardly anyone drove or walked the dead-end street, the old man had to be there. His defense was that porch-sitting was coded into his genes. End of debate.

Alex couldn't see either of them, but he could hear Lester calling out, "Dixie Cup. I'll get you a chair if you want."

"No that's fine, Mr. Bray, I'll stand."

"Suit yourself," he said, "long as you don't block my sunlight." He went on talking casually, commenting on the stupidity of having a slotted mailbox bolted onto the porch slab in this lily white neighborhood. And Alex had to admit, it was one of his mother's more neurotic moves. Nearly ten years ago she had worked herself into a frenzy over identity theft, so she hired some Goliath-looking guy to bolt a lock box onto their porch, and only she had the key.

The conversation fell to silence. Then Rebecca said, "I'm not sure how to say this." More silence, and then it sounded like Rebecca was crying. "You can't stay here," she said. "I am so sorry."

A bolt of guilt shot through Alex's chest. He wanted to take it all back. Just suck it up and see Dr. Kruger. Suddenly, once a month with the shrink seemed downright reasonable. All he had to do was march down the stairs and call it off.

"Now, now, Dixie Cup," Lester said. "Don't cry. It's all right."

"But it's not all right," she said. "I never should've put you here."

"Got to say, I'm a bit surprised. Was it the mother or the kid?"

Alex was on the verge of combustion.

"I shouldn't say anything." She paused, then spoke again. "It was Patricia. She thinks the stairs aren't safe. She's really worried about you."

"The hell she is," Lester said followed by a sharp guttural sound, like spitting. "No sense arguing about it."

"I've got to put my head together and find something better for you. I'll be making calls tonight."

"When do I need to leave?"

"Tomorrow afternoon," she said. "We've got a truck coming at four o'clock."

"You'll have a place for me by tomorrow at four? That's quick."

"Well...no, Mr. Bray. I don't think I'll have anything by then. Meantime, you'll probably have to stay in a nursing home. They've got respite beds for this sort of thing."

"I already told you, goddammit, no nursing homes! You'll have to drag me in by my dead body."

"Honestly," she said, "it would only be for a few days. I've got a list of families out there I'm sure would love to have you. It'll just take a little legwork."

"Then I'll be checking myself into a hotel till you find something satisfactory."

All Alex had to do was speak. Go down and correct the situation. Promise that his mother would change her mind. But he was frozen, left ear glued to the window screen.

"The agency doesn't expense hotel rooms," Rebecca said.

"I can pay for a damn room, got more money than I know what to do with. About time I spent it before the government gets its claws around it."

"Listen, Mr. Bray, I can't force you to do anything, but the only way for you to stay in our program is to follow the guidelines."

"You kicking me out?"

"No," Rebecca said.

"Then what are we doing?"

"We're coming to a compromise, Mr. Bray. I'll get the board to approve a hotel temporarily, at your expense. But I'll need to have one of our home health aides come look after you."

"You find me one half as pretty as you, and we've got ourselves a deal." He must have been studying her expression, because he went on to say, "That's better, Dixie Cup."

It sounded like pages turning. "You've got three doctor's appointments coming up. If you don't show for those, I will be sending you to a nursing home."

"You're a hard woman to shake," Lester said. "But you're an angel if ever I did see one. Now you go on and dig me up a good family. And a house with a decent front porch."

ALEX SAT on his bed slouched against the wall with his headphones on. His yearbook lay on his lap opened to a picture of the cross-country team. Next to the coach stood Britney Garrand, smiling unashamed, braces glistening, parabolic shadows under perky breasts. God, if he could be with her and not in this toxic house.

He began sketching upward from the waist, trading out her Delmar High T for a bikini top, adding maybe a cup size for the summer growing season. Just a little shading here, some curved lines there, and the result was perfection. The far more challenging mission was to draw her face as it appeared in the photo, replicating her smile and her personality. He couldn't say exactly why he liked her as much as he did, but the answer was right there in her face. If he could capture the essence of it in his drawing, he might discover the answer (even though he had tried all this before with the results ending up in his mother's shredder). The music was loud, but he had no idea what he was listening to. Lester's head popped into view. Alex startled. He pulled off his headphones.

"I knocked," Lester said. "But you didn't answer."

"Sorry, didn't hear you."

"You'll blow out your hearing with those things. Won't happen right away, but when you're my age you'll be sorry."

Alex shrugged and flipped the cover over his sketchpad.

"Came here to say goodbye. I'm not sure you're aware, but I'll be leaving tomorrow."

The taste of betrayal was overpowering. All Alex could say was, "Yeah, I wish you weren't."

"Me too, kid."

To show that he wasn't snooping, he asked, "Where will you go?"

"Can't say for sure. Think I'll get a room at the Hilton until something else comes through. I hear they got a nice breakfast and a pool with a Jacuzzi built right in." It was sad to picture Lester alone in a hotel, even a fancy one, when all he seemed to want was to live with a nice family.

Some kind of anti-gravitational force directed Alex's eyes to the map and the red thumbtack. It occurred to him that both he and Lester had important members of their family living far away. He sat up a little straighter. "What if you went back to Alabama?"

"I already told you, kid, there's no way."

"Your sister's got a whole house to herself, right?"

"No way in Hell could I live with her. I'd go crazy on top of all the shit that's already wrong with me."

"You could go for a visit." It was a long shot, popped right out of the park, but he had nothing to lose. "I could go with you." The thought of helping Lester return to his hometown seemed to appease his guilt.

Lester shook his head. "You got no business going down there."

"I know, but I was thinking I could hitch a ride the rest of the way down to Fort Lauderdale."

"You? Hitch a ride? That's nuts. Not to mention your mother. She'd have a goddamn fit."

"I wouldn't tell her."

"Oh that's great. Then I'd get arrested for kidnapping, spend my final days in a jail cell."

"Only if she pressed charges," Alex said. "And I don't think she would."

Lester's body wavered, like he was fending off a shifting breeze. "I'll humor you, kid. Why wouldn't she press charges?"

"Because she couldn't take the negative publicity." Alex rose from his bed and stared at the map. He had read somewhere that if you visualized an outcome strongly enough, and you believed in your vision, you could make it a reality. That's why he'd put the map there in the first place, and it was finally paying off. He could feel it.

"You may have a point there," Lester said. "But I'm too old, and you can't drive. So the whole thing's moot."

"I can drive," Alex said, trying to sound believable.

"Listen, kid, I only came here to say goodbye. You'll have to find some other way to make it down there. For your sake, I hope you do."

CHAPTER SEVEN

A metallic squeak and a couple of voices penetrated through the barrier of Alex's sleep. He lifted his head off the pillow and recognized the sounds.

"Oh God, oh God, oh God," he could hear. It was his mother getting banged by Bill. An awful howl rose out of Bill, followed by different sounds, canine and otherwise.

Then Alex heard Lester muttering profanity in the next room. It made him wonder why anyone would want to live in this house. The deal he had made with his mother was probably in Lester's best interests. With that guilt-reducing thought in mind, he drifted back to sleep.

But it didn't last. A slight knock on his door. Then the door opened.

"Hush," Lester whispered. "If your offer's still good, we'll leave in the morning."

"Definitely," Alex said.

"We'll go to Alabama," Lester said. He was like a black phantom crouched over Alex's bed. "Then we'll see your dad in Florida."

"Sounds good," Alex said.

Then the phantom was gone.

THERE WAS no way Alex was going to sleep after that. He sat at his computer and, courtesy of his mother's gift card, downloaded about fifty songs onto his iPod. Then he grabbed his duffel bag and started packing it with clothes and drawing materials. He tossed in a medium-quality sketchpad and the new leather case Bill had given him for his birthday. Inside were three grades of lead, a mechanical pencil, sharpener, charcoals, erasers and a can of fixative spray. He was making a bit of noise, which made him worry about his mother barging in. So he stopped, slid the bag under his bed and remained still until morning light.

There were voices and commotion, and then the garage door opened beneath him. He rose out of bed and went over to the window. His mother and Bill were gone.

A knock on the wall. "Hey, kid." It was Lester.

Alex plopped his duffel bag onto the bed. "I'm packing."

Downstairs, Lester was sitting at the dining room table, a bowl of cereal at his left and a map spread out before him. He wore reading glasses that hung out near the end of his nose. But instead of making him look silly, the glasses gave him a bookish appearance. Without looking away, he said, "She comes back, we'll have some explaining to do."

"Don't worry," Alex said, pumped with excitement. "She never leaves work early." He pulled out a box of Golden Grahams. "Where'd you get the map?"

"The Caddy—got the whole country in there." He looked up and took off his glasses. "Find me a yellow highlighter, if you would."

"No problem," Alex said. "I've got my bag ready."

"Me too. You carry mine down." Lester paused for a moment. Then he said, "You need to write a note to your mother. Tell her you went willingly. Tell her you'll call on a regular basis. And tell her you love her."

Alex looked away. "I might skip that last part."

"Nope," Lester said. "You put it in or we don't go."

THEIR FIRST stop was a Key Bank where Lester apparently kept a lot of money. Alex watched as the old man filled out a cash slip in the amount of eleven hundred dollars. Then he instructed the teller to give him nothing but hundred dollar bills. "Easier on my backside," he said.

Lester slid the bills into his wallet, slipped the wallet into his back pocket and made a slow trek to the Cadillac. As they pulled out of the parking lot, Alex timidly said, "I can't take money out of my college fund without my mom's signature. I won't be able to pay for much."

"Now you tell me," Lester said. "You invite me on a trip. Then you expect me to pay for everything. That's how you operate?"

Alex didn't know what to say.

Lester smiled. "I'm busting your chops, kid. I've got more money than I know what to do with." It was the same line he'd given Rebecca.

"I could help you with that problem," Alex said.

"I'm sure you could, and I'm sure you will."

For Alex, the official start of the trip happened when they passed the Thruway tollgate heading west on I-88. The day was colorless, a world gone graphite, but this had no effect on Alex's mood. Not only was he thrilled about the possibilities ahead, he was also relieved of his guilt over Lester. How could he be accused of abandoning the old man if he was sitting right next to him?

But if Lester was excited, he didn't exactly put on a parade about it. He just sat there and drove wordlessly—no radio, nothing. Maybe it was a secret test of endurance. Who could stay silent the longest? Who would crack?

Southbound on I-81, they brushed the eastern side of Binghamton and crossed the state line into Pennsylvania. It was a hundred miles since either of them had spoken.

When Lester finally broke the silence, it came with the chill of reality. He cleared his throat and said, "You sure you know how to drive?"

Alex didn't say anything. It was too soon to be having this conversation. Way too soon, because they were close enough to turn around and be home before anyone knew better.

"I asked you a question," Lester said.

Alex finally responded. "I'm trying to figure a way to answer it."

"Don't tell me you don't know how to drive!"

"Actually, I don't. I sort of...lied."

"That's not funny." Lester made a fist of his right hand. "You may be a better liar than I thought."

"Sorry," Alex said, "I thought it was the only way to convince you."

"Goddamn right!"

"I've got a permit. I swear." Alex pulled out his wallet then proudly held up his brand new license card.

"All right, put that away." Lester flashed a mean look. "Jesus, now I'll have to teach you how to drive."

"I don't think I'll need much training."

"You can't know until you're behind the wheel. But it's pretty simple, especially with this car. Everything's automatic. Long as you're not mentally defective or a nervous wreck, you should learn just fine."

"When do we start?" Alex asked. "I'm ready."

"Hold your britches, kid. I'm an old man, and I'm tired. I need a place to rest."

LESTER CHOSE a truck stop south of Hazelton and parked at the edge of the lot. All the windows were down. He lay on the backseat with his hands draped over his crotch, legs pretzeled against the door. To remain like that, in a raspy state of sleep for over an hour, seemed pretty amazing.

Alex was afraid to leave him there, afraid the old man might choke on his own spit, afraid some outlaw redneck might pry open the trunk and take their stuff. But the power of boredom gradually took hold. He got out of the car and made his way up through a tangle of new growth trees. He stopped at a point where he could still see the Cadillac and the L-shaped parking lot. On the other side of the ridge, down below, lay a broad expanse of grass and both directions of busy interstate. Beyond that was a strip mine, making the distant horizon raw and ugly.

A path separated the top of the ridge. Alex followed it about fifty yards to a graffiti-riddled boulder and a pile of bottles and dented beer cans. He turned back to the path's origin and spotted something unusual. It was a shiny stick propped against a young maple. The stick was speckled with tiny knots, but it was nearly straight. Someone had used it as a walking stick and must have left it accidentally. He checked its feel. It was solid but not too heavy. He decided he'd give it to Lester.

The first thing he noticed when he approached the Cadillac was that the windows were all raised. He looked through the glare. The old man was gone, probably in the bathroom. Alex perched himself on the back bumper and examined the stick. It was definitely a good find.

"Where the hell you been?" It was Lester gasping for air, leaning against a blue Odyssey.

"Sorry," Alex said. "I just went for a little hike."

"You had me worried to death." He took a few awkward steps closer. "Who the hell hikes at a truck stop?"

"Sorry." Alex walked toward the old man eager to show off the stick.

"Thought you might've hitched a ride with some trucker, or got taken by some trucker."

"Nothing like that," Alex said. "But I did find this stick." He raised it with both hands. "I thought you could use it."

"I don't need a goddamn stick. I can walk fine." Lester squared himself in front Alex, stared for few seconds then grabbed the stick. He walked between the Cadillac and a PT Cruiser, and he launched the stick javelin-style into the grass.

Then he grabbed at his chest. He let out an awful moan and lurched forward against the Cadillac's hood.

"Kid," he managed to say. "I need my nitro."

Alex leaped forward and propped Lester up by his armpits. "What's that?"

Lester was gasping. "It's a little brown bottle. In my bag...get it now."

Alex lowered the old man to the pavement, took the keys out of his hand and darted back to the trunk. He popped it open then rifled through the musty suitcase. There was a black toiletry bag stuffed with medicine bottles.

"Hurry," Lester said.

"I got it! I got it!" Alex twisted open a tiny glass bottle and tapped five or six white tablets onto his palm. He knelt in front of the old man.

"I just need one," Lester said. "Put it in my mouth, under my tongue."

Alex stuck a tablet under Lester's raised tongue, which looked all purple and nasty. "There," he said, "I got it in." He put the rest of the pills back in the bottle and capped it.

Lester closed his eyes and lowered his head. His hands had dropped from his chest down to the center of his belly. "I'll be okay," he said. "Just help me into the car. I need some water."

Alex opened the driver's door and guided Lester to the seat. Then he ran. He actually ran to the glass entry doors of the truck stop to the wall of chilled beverages.

On his sprint back to the car, he couldn't help but equate the black Cadillac to a hearse. "God, please be alive," he said. He was actually praying. He slid into the passenger seat. "Here's the water. I got three bottles."

Lester put his hand forward and nodded. His nods were usually deliberate. This one wavered.

Alex put a bottle in the old man's hand. "Here, drink it up."

Lester leaned back and drank a small amount. Then he set the bottle into the center console. "I'll be okay, kid."

Alex couldn't stop it. He felt a surge of tears.

"No reason to cry," Lester said. "I'm an old goat, should've never tossed that stick."

"I shouldn't have left for so long."

Lester took another sip and then said, "Well, you're right about that. Next time, you're either in the car or in the building. Don't go off hiking without telling me first."

"Yes, sir."

"You know, I was thinking," Lester said. "Might not be such a bad idea for me to have a walking stick."

Alex smiled and said, "Don't move. I'll get it."

THEY WERE silent again for the next stretch of interstate, but it was a different silence than before. To ease Lester's burden, it would have been an ideal time for Alex to drive, but he just sat there feeling useless. His thoughts had shifted from all the possibilities awaiting him down in Florida to Lester and whether he could even make it to the next rest stop. And what if he actually died?

"You're looking at me funny, kid."

"What do you mean?"

"You keep glancing over at me, like I'm wearing a vest of explosives."

"I was just wondering," Alex said. "Shouldn't we go to the hospital?"

"Most definitely not," Lester said. "They'd only torture me and add more pills to my collection."

"Was it a heart attack?"

"Nah, just a spell of angina. Doesn't happen that often. Don't you worry."

But Alex was beyond worried. He remembered how his mother had said Lester was too medically unstable to drive and shouldn't take the wheel until he was cleared by a doctor. Now here he was, driving over seventy miles an hour in heavy traffic.

"Listen, kid," Lester said. "If it makes you feel any better, we'll go to Florida first. Then we'll hit Alabama on the return trip. How's that sound?"

"Why would you want to do that?" Alex said. "You don't even know anyone down there."

"You got me curious about your father. Wouldn't want to delay that meeting."

"It's okay with me," Alex said. Huge understatement. If the old man coded out on the road, he should at least have the decency to do it after the Florida leg of their trip.

Traffic intensified. It was rush hour in Harrisburg. Lester kept the Cadillac in the slow lane and let about a dozen motorists pass by. "All these people in a hurry to get home," he said. Then he looked over and caught Alex fiddling with his nose. "That's disgusting."

"What?" Alex said, lowering his hand.

"You wipe any snot on my interior, and you can walk the rest of the way down to Fort Lauderdale."

"I wouldn't want to waste it," Alex said. "This is home-grown snack food." He was kidding, wondering how the old man would take it.

"That's a foul habit. You ought to stop doing it, especially if you plan on meeting a nice girl. She'll drop you quicker than a hot potato."

"What if she eats hers too?" He could barely keep a straight face.

"Oh, you're asking for it now," Lester said. "Think of all the crap you breathe in through your nose. Then you eat it. It's like eating from a pool skimmer."

"Nice visual," Alex said. "But, for the record, I don't eat boogers and I pledge not to soil your car with them."

Lester shook his head. "You had me, kid."

"Serves you right for staring at me instead of looking at the road."

Anybody ever call you a smart-ass?"

"You're the first."

"Ha," Lester said, smiling broadly. And somehow that smile made him look healthier.

CHAPTER EIGHT

From a geographic standpoint, the best part of the trip came next. After all those hours cutting through Pennsylvania, the interstate quickly sliced through an appendage of Maryland then crossed the easternmost limb of West Virginia. A moment later, they passed the state line into Virginia. The transition from state to state made it feel like progress on a grand scale.

The skies were darkening, especially off to the east. Next town ahead was Winchester. "Let's stop here and get a room." Lester poked a thumb at his chest. "This old sack of bones needs a break."

They pulled into a Hampton Inn, nestled between a Christian college and a shopping mall. Alex went inside and checked for room availability while Lester remained in the car. The desk clerk had said there were plenty of rooms, which Alex proudly relayed back to Lester.

The old man was looking at his walking stick. "With separate beds?" he asked.

"I didn't check, but I think so."

"Kid, I told you to ask for a non-smoking room with separate beds. Now how the hell hard is that?"

"Sorry," Alex said. "I'll check again."

Their room was on the second floor overlooking the parking lot and a corner of college. Alex flipped through channels on the TV while Lester stood at the window with a bottle of water. One by one, he downed his allotment of evening pills. "Right around here," he said, "is where the bulk of the Civil War was fought." He took his last capsule. "The end result of all that madness is Christian colleges and shopping malls."

"Sounds like a fair trade-off," Alex said.

Lester laughed a little, which was good to hear. Then he said, "Maybe you're right, kid."

They took turns using the bathroom. Lester shut off the nightstand light. "Sleep well, kid. You've got a driving lesson tomorrow."

THE SUN wasn't even all the way up, but Lester was out of bed and maneuvering himself around the room, switching on every lamp and spreading the curtain wide. "Rise and shine, kid."

Like most mornings, Alex awakened with a stiff dick, which had nothing to do with a dream or a fantasy. Just his body's way of saluting the new day. Usually he didn't mind. Today was different. He sat up with the bedspread draped over his lap, waiting for the erection to die down. Lester sat across on the other bed, reading a section of the complimentary *USA Today*. Figuring it was safe, Alex cupped his hands over his boxers and started for the bathroom.

"Meet you downstairs for breakfast," Lester said.

"Sounds good."

"And no whacking off." He rolled up the newspaper and pointed it toward Alex's groin. "We got us a tight itinerary."

Alex blushed his way to the bathroom.

The hotel lobby had a self-serve breakfast bar stocked with enough food for a serious binge. Alex ambled his way around the U-shaped bar, loading up his plate with biscuits and sausage gravy, scrambled eggs, a blueberry yogurt and a chocolate muffin. He could hear a group of old people with Southern accents recounting their drive along the Blue Ridge Parkway all the way up from Asheville. Next table over was Lester sitting alone eating a bowl of instant oatmeal. He put his newspaper on his lap to make room for Alex's tray.

As Alex sat down, the group stopped talking. In fact, the whole lobby was quiet.

"Guess we make quite a pair," Lester said, loudly enough for the other diners to hear. Then, just as quickly, the crowd started talking again like nothing happened.

Alex looked around and whispered, "I feel like I'm on camera."

"Get used to it," Lester said. "We're south of the Mason Dixon. Last time I was around here, interracial mixing was about as common as sushi bars."

"You mean Southerners don't like sushi?"

Lester laughed then pointed to Alex's tray. "You got enough there for a small village."

Alex nodded as he forked a saturated piece of biscuit.

"Hope you don't have a nervous stomach. I don't want you vomiting all over my interior." It occurred to Alex that Lester would have been in far better shape if he'd taken care of himself as well as his blessed Cadillac.

"I can handle it," Alex said. But since he'd never driven before, he wasn't completely sure. He set aside the muffin and yogurt. Meanwhile Lester went up to the front desk and took care of the bill.

"FIGURE WE got about an hour before the mall opens," Lester said from the driver's seat. They were sitting at a red light. "We'll use the parking lot for your first lesson. You need to get a feel for the car." Except for a few vehicles scattered about, the mall parking lot was a desert of asphalt and yellow lines. Lester drove to a remote spot near a concrete lamppost. He cut the engine and opened his door. "Time to switch," he said, handing over the keys.

Alex got in the driver's seat and started the engine.

"Adjust your mirrors." Lester pointed to the toggle controlling the side mirrors.

Alex made the adjustments. His nerves were starting to kick in.

"Next thing is the transmission," Lester said. "Hold down your brake pedal and shift her into drive."

"I know how to do that."

"Well then, do it."

Alex pulled the lever and stepped on the gas. The car leaped forward. He hit the brake. There was a loud screech. In his periphery, he could see Lester's head pitch forward and back.

"Sorry," Alex said.

"It's all right. You'll be lousy for a while until you learn."

"What am I doing wrong?"

"First thing, you got a big block V-8 sitting in front of you with enough torque to snap your neck. Go gentle on the gas."

"Okay."

"Second, you got power brakes. Go easy on'em. Skid and you lose control."

"Okay."

"Do it again. Gentle on the gas, gentle on the brake."

Alex let go of the brake and allowed the car to run on idle. The speedometer registered ten miles an hour.

"A little faster," Lester said.

The car bucked forward. Alex hit the brakes causing the tires to screech. "Jesus, I suck."

"Easy does it. You'll get it." Lester pointed to a lamppost about a quarter mile away. "Go up to the access road and park in front of that pole. Without hitting it."

"I'll try," Alex said.

"Trying is worthless. Just go for it and see what happens."

"You're not worried about your car?"

Lester didn't respond right away. He reached forward and laid his hand on the dashboard. "Tell you what," he finally said, "I'll make you a deal."

Alex took his hands off the wheel. His right foot kept the car from moving. He thought of his mother's deal just a few days earlier and how that was working out—not too bad, actually. "What kind of a deal?" he said.

"You get her parked successfully in front of that pole, and the car's yours." He paused then said, "After I die, that is."

"What if the car dies before you?"

"I wouldn't bet on that. But let's just say if she does, you get the scrap value."

"I think I'd rather have you around," Alex said.

"That's nice. Now let's move before the damn mall opens."

Alex eased his foot into the gas. The car worked its way up to twenty-five miles an hour. He backed off as they approached the access road.

"Treat it like a stop sign," Lester said.

A small jolt and the car came to a stop.

"Good," Lester said. "Look both ways and get on the road when it's clear."

"But it's always clear."

"Let's say there's a big Mack truck coming this way." He motioned toward the left lane. "And a Corvette coming up from the right. You got just enough time to cross in front of the truck and get in past the Vette."

Alex inched the car forward and turned onto the lane.

"Pow!" Lester yelled. "We just got crunched between the car and truck. We're dead."

"What do you mean?"

"Listen, kid; when you commit to a course of action, don't hesitate. Don't limp-dick yourself into a hole. Don't drive that way, and don't live that way. Now bring her back around."

The second time went a lot smoother. Instead of being sandwiched, according to Lester, they were only honked at and given the finger by both drivers.

"Do it again," Lester said.

Alex circled back to the intersection. "There's the truck, there's the car," he said. "I'm going." He pressed the gas pedal and turned onto the lane knowing this time how the engine would respond.

"Good job, kid. Now go to the pole."

It took him three tries to get the car squarely into the parking spot. On his second attempt, he tapped the pole with the front bumper, prompting a loud "Jesus Christ!" from Lester. But the third try was smooth.

"Good," Lester said. "Now back her into the same spot. And don't rely on your mirrors."

A white Ford Escape pulled up and parked along Lester's side of the Cadillac. A man in a security uniform stepped out and walked around to Alex's side. Lester shot Alex a serious look and said, "Open your window but let me do the talking."

The security guard placed a pudgy hand on Alex's side-view mirror. "Mind telling me what you're doing here?" The man was muscularly built, but his voice had a high, effeminate quality.

Lester said, "Just a little driving lesson. When the mall opens, we'll be gone."

The guard squatted low enough to look directly at Lester. "Problem is, your boy here smacked that pole pretty good. I'll have to fill out an incident report."

Lester said, "That's a load of crap. He barely touched it."

"You can step out of the car, sir. See for yourself."

"Kill the engine," Lester said to Alex. "I'll have myself a look." He held onto the doorframe and pulled himself out of the car.

The security guard met him at the pole. "See right here?" he said, pointing to a dark line on concrete.

"That's nothing," Lester said. "These things get tapped fifty times a day." He looked back at Alex and gave a thumbs-up, as if everything was perfectly fine. To the guard he said, "That's why the goddamn things are made of reinforced concrete!"

"Sir, I don't appreciate that. I'm just trying to do my job by the book."

"Screw the book," Lester said. "There's no damage here. Let us be."

The guard looked down at the Cadillac's front license plate and said, "Is that how they teach you to talk in New York?"

"Yes they do. It's called Common Sense 101. You ought to enroll yourself." Using the front fender for support, Lester walked over to Alex and said, "Lesson's over, let's go."

The guard remained still, arms crossed over his inflated chest. "Other thing is," he said. "The mall's not insured for driving lessons. I'm inclined to have you arrested for unlawful use of public property."

And I'm inclined to get you fired," Lester said as he readjusted the mirrors and started the engine, "for sexual harassment."

"What on earth are you talking about?"

"I didn't exactly like the way you grabbed my ass when I got out of the car."

"You're a crazy old man."

"Maybe so, but your supervisor may think otherwise."

"Just get out of here." The guard pointed to an exit lane. "Go back to New York."

Lester put the car in drive, tapped the pole, backed up and then sped out of the parking lot.

Alex broke into a spasm of nervous laughter.

"What the hell's so funny?" Lester said.

"You are. That was insane."

And then Lester began laughing. "Yeah, that was kind of stupid," he said. "I should've just said, 'I'm real sorry, sir,' and be done with it."

"You don't think he'll come after us?"

"Hell no."

Alex smiled. "So I didn't do too badly, my first lesson?"

"No, kid, you did fine. And I didn't forget about our deal. Once I'm gone, the car's yours." He put his hand toward Alex.

"I hope that's not for a long time," Alex said, shaking Lester's hand.

"I'd like a little more time too."

CHAPTER NINE

Alex was starting to think Virginia would go on forever. Not being allowed to drive didn't help. He needed another lesson under his belt, Lester had said, before he was ready to contend with the interstate. So he sat there feeling bored, alternating between map-reading, snacking, listening to his iPod and sketching the never-ending ridge running parallel to the road. But bored was better than scared. And there was a lot to be afraid of. Number One on the list was the old man dying on the road. Number Two was that his mother would press charges, leading to a nationwide manhunt for him and Lester. Number Three was old and familiar. It was that, after all his efforts, his father would still reject him. Fear Number Three would loom larger and larger the closer they got to Fort Lauderdale.

They stopped for gas and snacks in Roanoke. Back in the car, Lester said, "You look a little down, kid. What's on your mind?"

"Nothing really, it's a long state."

"You wait till we hit Florida. Son of a bitch is like its own country."

"The scenery any better?"

"Nope, it's worse. Flatter than plywood. If something looks like a hill, it's either a landfill or some crazy amusement park. And all there is to see are ridiculous billboards. Least that's how I remember it."

"You think it's changed much?"

"Nothing stays the same." Lester bit off a piece of mozzarella stick and chewed it slowly. Then he went on a rant about global warming—how a good percentage of Florida would be underwater in fifty years, how anyone with brains would avoid purchasing coastal property, how those same smart people would do well to take scuba lessons, and how the paid-off politicians in Washington would never rise to meet the challenges ahead. And then, for no good reason, the old man started talking about death.

Alex kept saying, "Uh-huh" when it seemed to fit, but his mind barely registered. He was focusing on the road sign for Blacksburg and Virginia Tech—five miles ahead. A South Korean student named Seung-Hui Cho had gone on a shooting rampage, killing thirty-two people before taking his own pathetic life. Alex pointed and said, "Speaking of death."

"Goddamn crazed psychopath son of a bitch," Lester said. "Worst peacetime massacre in the history of this country." He went on talking about the toxic mess some people had become and how they'd ruin civilization for everyone else. But all Alex could think about was Dr. Kruger and his accusation. Angry, male, loner. The sting was still there. But as he thought about the idea of actually carrying a lethal weapon to school, he realized he could no more go on a killing spree than he could defy the law of gravity or give birth to a child. Although he wouldn't mind smashing his fist into Dr. Kruger's face.

ONE THING you did not mess with was Lester's afternoon ritual.

Naptime. The old man parked the car under the partial shade of a birch tree in Statesville, North Carolina. To save gas, he turned off the engine, apparently unfazed by the sticky heat and unconcerned about Alex's comfort level.

Lester had been napping on the backseat for nearly an hour while Alex sat in the front passenger seat bored and a little agitated. A bundle of clouds like gargantuan plums approached from the west, and a fresh breeze was gathering. The first raindrops were cool and pleasant. But then, almost immediately, it was a monsoon.

Alex cranked the engine and raised all the windows, hoping Lester would finally wake up. But the old man kept snoring. It took an act of God to finally get his attention. A bolt of lightening. Then a rib-splitting crack of thunder.

Lester worked his way up to a seated position. He twisted himself in both directions. Then he clicked on his seatbelt.

"What are you doing?" Alex asked.

"I'm buckling up. This is your second driving lesson."

"But it's raining hard."

"So?" Lester said. "You can't drive in the rain?"

"No, I mean, yeah. I can drive. But I thought you said I wasn't ready for the interstate."

"You're not. You're going to drive up and down the streets of this Podunk town till I say you are."

"Don't you want to sit up front?"

"I can see fine back here. Let's get her moving."

Alex fumbled around the dash and steering column for the wiper switch. He found it and turned it to its highest setting. Then he switched on the lights but still couldn't see more than twenty feet in front of the hood. Nonetheless, he shifted the car into drive but kept his foot on the brake. It was an avalanche of rain outside. He let the car idle its way to the nearest intersection. "What now?" he asked, chest pounding.

"Pick a direction and go with it. No hesitation. But the roads are wet, so go easy on the brake and easy on the gas."

"Anything else?"

"Yeah, don't hit anything."

Alex could barely make out the sign, but guessed it said Green Street. He watched for a gap in oncoming traffic, made the decision and steered left. There were cars parked intermittently along the right side of the road. It would be easy, incredibly easy, to slam into any of them. He veered out to the center of the street. Headlights approached from the oncoming side.

"Careful, kid, give him room."

It turned out to be a van, and it sprayed a gusher of additional water onto the windshield. He hit the brake, causing the car to fishtail. "Oh shit," he said.

"Let go of the brake!" Lester yelled. "Don't over-steer."

Alex pulled his foot away from the brake, but the car kept sliding. "Slow her down gently."

He eased back into the pedal. The car regained a straight line— straight toward the back of a low-rider pickup truck. The Cadillac stopped a few inches shy of the bumper. "God, that was close." His chest was seismic.

"If that truck's tailgate was down," Lester said, "we'd have a nice chunk taken out of the radiator."

Alex was shaking. He put the transmission in park. "You wanna take over?"

"Hell no, I'm not getting outside in that crap. You're doing all right."

"I don't feel so good."

"Shake it off. Remember what I said. When it's wet, go easy on the brake and easy on the gas. And always be aware of the other guy."

"I almost hit a parked car."

"Almost doesn't count," Lester said.

Alex backed away from the pickup and eased into the lane. He decided he didn't like Green Street anymore, so he took a right onto Sharpe, which also had a fair number of parked cars. *Easy on the brake, easy on the gas*, he replayed in his mind along with, *don't over-steer.*

After a few blocks, his withered confidence seemed to renew itself. The rain had lessened to an annoying drizzle. He switched the wipers to low. He was officially a driver. "How am I doing?" he asked.

"Fine, kid, take a right up here. We'll work our way out to the interstate."

The word *interstate* was all it took to throw him back into a bundle of nerves. He passed through the center of town, which was probably charming, but all he could focus on was the road and the signs leading to I-77.

"Think you're ready?" Lester asked.

"Yeah, I think so."

"Well, there it is." He pointed right. "Southbound ramp. Hop on and speed her up. Don't wimp your way onto the highway."

"What do you mean?"

"You've got to match the speed of the other drivers and merge your way in. Nothing's worse than timid drivers slowing their way into traffic."

Alex pumped the accelerator, felt the rush of eight cylinders and the compression of leather seat against his back. "How fast?" he asked.

"Get her up past sixty. If it's clear, get in. If not, adjust your speed up or down and find an opening. Use your signal."

He was so riddled with fear that all he heard was sixty and signal. He flicked the blinker, checked his speed and merged in behind a white Volvo. His nerves started to ease. "Now what?"

"When it's clear, like right now, get her up to seventy-two. That's what I drive. It's always been fast enough for me."

Traffic picked up, and the road converted to four lanes as they made their way into pre-rush-hour Charlotte. Alex bit the inside skin under his lip. Skyscrapers cut into his left periphery, but he didn't risk taking his eyes off the congested road, which funneled down to three lanes, multiple mergers and a spaghetti of overpasses. A beat-up Winnebago kept their speed down to fifty. "Should I change lanes?"

"If you want," Lester said. "Watch your blind spot. Make sure you got plenty of room."

Alex pressed the blinker, checked the left lane, waited for two cars to pass then eased his way over. Pretty smooth, he thought. It was his first successful lane change in heavy traffic—a monumental achievement. He could hold his own among all these other drivers. Hell, if Lester let him, he could take the wheel all the way down to Florida.

"Turn off your damn blinker," Lester said.

ALEX HAD driven them past Columbia, South Carolina, when Lester abruptly called it a day. "We stop here," he said, "this exit." There was a strange urgency to his voice, and it didn't take long to figure out why. Lester pointed to the first motel off the interstate, which looked far less desirable than the two or three hotels just up the road. Alex parked by the lobby entrance, and Lester immediately got out. There was a circle of wetness on the old man's pants. Alex looked away, initially feeling repulsed but then incredibly sad.

Lester made his way around the Cadillac toward the brightly lit lobby as if nothing was wrong. The back of his pants was a lot worse than the front. For cover, Alex followed closely behind. Lester didn't say a single thing until he got to the front desk and pulled out his wallet, which fortunately appeared to be dry. He signed for the room and took an envelope with two key cards.

Back outside Lester said, "You park the car. I'll meet you in the room." He handed Alex one of the cards. "Bring in my bag."

The best thing about the motel was that you could drive right up to the room door. Lester was already in the bathroom taking a shower. He had left a twenty dollar bill under the door, which seemed strange until the old man started barking orders over the noise of the shower. "Take the money. Go next door to that restaurant—the one lit up like Vegas. Get yourself something, and bring me a chicken sandwich, plenty of mayo."

Alex did as instructed. To make it easy on himself, he ordered two identical sandwiches, two Snapple teas and then added a large order of onion rings. The food came out hot and smelling like a grease fire. As he cut across the parking lot, he was a little afraid of what he might find back in the room. But his fear passed when he looked over at the far bed. There was Lester in shiny black pajamas with gold pinstripes, looking like African royalty while he watched a baseball game between the Braves and Mets. He got out of bed and made his way to the rickety table. "Smells good," he said. "Let's dig in."

"Hope you like onion rings," Alex said, feeling a little giddy about the day's accomplishments. "I got about a pound of 'em."

"How could anyone not like onion rings?"

"My mother hates them. She calls them uncivilized."

Lester unwrapped his sandwich and took a bite. Then he looked at Alex and said, "That reminds me, you need to call her tonight."

And, just like that, the mood was ruined.

CHAPTER TEN

The baseball game lasted through dinner and was now in the bottom of the sixth tied at two runs apiece, but the on-field drama wasn't enough to hold Lester's interest. He was asleep and snoring.

No way was Alex going to call his mother. For one, he didn't want to deal with the inevitable tirade over who's the boss and who's only sixteen and who the hell did he think he was, blah blah blah. The other reason not to call was traceability. She'd see South Carolina and pretty much know where he was headed. But for Lester's sake, Alex needed to make it look like the call was made on the motel invoice. He picked up the phone, got an outside line and dialed one of the few 518 numbers he had committed to memory.

The phone rang and a female voice said, "Delmar Pizza, can you hold?"

"Sure," Alex said. Holding was good. Stretch it out. He looked over at Lester. Still sleeping.

"Pick up or delivery?"

"Um, actually I just wanted to know your hours, like when do you close?"

"Eleven o'clock."

"So when would be the absolute latest I could order a pizza and wings?" It was the kind of information that could come in handy someday.

"I wouldn't order past 10:30, personally. I can take your order now and have it ready by eleven."

"No, that's okay." He didn't want them wasting food on his behalf. "I'll call back."

"Whatever," she said.

"Same to you," he responded and hung up the phone. Lester was either still asleep or a hell of a good faker.

ALEX WOKE to the sound of retching. He looked over at Lester's sleeping body and figured the noise was coming from the next room. Some sick man was puking his guts out. Alex looked over at the clock—4:32 A.M. A toilet flush replaced the sound of vomiting. Then there was moaning.

"Son of a bitch," Lester said. He pulled himself up, switched on the nearest wall lamp and staggered to the bathroom. "No sleeping through that nonsense." He turned to Alex. "Let's check out and get on the road."

Alex popped out of bed. "Think we can make it all the way to Fort Lauderdale?"

"It's still quite a ways. But with both of us driving, we should."

They were gassed up and on the interstate by 5:30, Lester first to drive. "Despite that rude awakening," he said, "I slept pretty well. Fact, I must've slept right through your talk with your mother. How'd it go?"

"Not so good," Alex said. "She told me she knows where we're going, and she threatened to press charges. I don't think I'll call her again." He didn't want to have to call Delmar Pizza again either.

Lester didn't say anything for a while. He had a deep contemplative look—furrowed brow, pursed lips, both hands on the wheel. Finally, he said, "Used to be, sixteen meant something. When I was your age, I spent my summers loading and unloading boxcars at a rail yard fourteen hours a day. Worked afternoons during the school year and saved enough for college."

"That's a lot of money."

"Wasn't as much then. My point is you ought to be responsible for yourself, earlier the better. I won't make you call her."

"I still don't think she'll press charges."

"May not matter one way or the other."

"Why's that?"

"All depends on what the age of consent is for driving cross-country with an ancient black man. And I don't know what that is."

Alex didn't know either. His hunch was that his mother wouldn't put herself under negative public scrutiny. But his remedy, if she did press charges, would be to call every media outlet in the Capital District and explain how she had kicked Lester out of their house before calling him a kidnapper. That's what Alex would do. He'd do his part to ruin her political future, and he wouldn't feel bad about it in the least.

As they passed a sign with a peach and an Olympic flame welcoming them into Georgia, Lester talked about the old rail yard in his hometown of Terrell, Alabama. He said it was the lifeblood of the community, like GE had been in Schenectady before all the layoffs.

But then, in 1968, the rail yard closed and the town practically folded. Lester's dad, who'd been a functional alcoholic before the closing, turned into a fall-down drunk. He died in 1971 of liver failure.

"He never learned to appreciate what he had," Lester said. "Never found a way to pick himself back up."

"Did you like him?" Alex wanted to know.

"Tough question. I think every son wants to like his dad, give him the highest benefit of the doubt. I suppose that's what I did." He flashed a knowing look. "And that's what you're doing right now."

It was probably true, and it made Alex wonder how any human with a pulse could measure up to the expectations he had built. Even with all the bashing over the years by his mother, there still remained a protective shell around his father. That shell was built with excuses, none too far fetched. As a little boy, Alex had pictured his father tirelessly trying to find him, but the man was so far away that he'd forgotten how to get home. Then there was the excuse that his father was just waiting for the right moment, a big party moment— Surprise!—and it could happen anytime. When it kept not happening, Alex hit upon the witness protection program. Which held for a long time until Google threw everything out of balance. But even now, without a workable pretext, Alex clung to the idea that his father was still a good man.

"It's good to hope for the best about a person," Lester said. "But don't let it fool you. It's not all milk and honey."

Alex tilted his head. "Milk and honey?" The old man had some ridiculous sayings.

"You know what I mean. You got some dark business with regard to your father. Don't cover it up. Because that's where your truth is."

Alex had grown used to hearing advice, typically in two formats: the politically correct crap he got from his mother or the psychobabble crap he got from Dr. Kruger. This particular advice from Lester felt more authentic. He'd try to remember it for later.

It was time for lunch. Lester pulled into a truck stop just outside the coastal town of Brunswick. The parking lot was so crowded that even the handicapped spots were taken. They had to park a good forty yards from the building.

Lester opened his door and said, "I got a mind to use that stick."

Alex reached behind his seat. "Here you go." It felt good to be of service. In fact, the whole day had a good feeling about it.

The old man huffed and hobbled his way across the parking lot, pausing once to catch his breath and once more to swat at a militia of white gnats. His final stop came at the set of glass entry doors. "Patience, kid," he said.

It looked like a supermarket inside, but beyond the aisles of merchandise there was a restaurant with two buffet peninsulas loaded with food. Soups and salad fixings, meats and side dishes. For dessert, there was an assortment of cobblers and a soft-serve ice cream machine with three chrome handles. Alex surveyed the abundance before him. Except for the collard greens, he wanted everything.

"Don't you stuff yourself," Lester said. "You're driving next." He turned to the hostess and told her they'd both have the buffet. Then, to Alex, he said, "Fill me a plate, if you would. I'll take a salad with Thousand Island and a thick slice of that roast beef. I'm headed for the bathroom."

Alex moved around the bustle of people with a tray, piling food onto plates. Then he looked around for a table. He scanned the well-populated dining room, hesitating at the far corner booth where a pony-tailed woman was sporting a spandex halter top. She was sitting alone. His heart swelled.

He made his way to the round table nearest her booth. This day kept getting better. He positioned himself in such a way that his eyes, his main entrée plate and the woman's breasts all existed along the same Euclidian plane. He set Lester's plate to the left.

It takes a degree of skill to simultaneously eat and stare while trying not to be too obvious. The V of her top revealed a gulf of cleavage. He took a bite of mashed potatoes and looked again. He could feel himself getting hard. It was unstoppable.

"Why don't you take a picture?" the woman said. "It'll last longer."

Snagged! His face felt as hot as the mashed potatoes.

A muscular man with tattoos on his forearms put a plate down and sat across from the woman. But she didn't even look at him. She kept staring at Alex, giving him a taste of his own behavior.

Alex smiled nervously while starting on a piece of batter-fried chicken breast.

The man turned and looked at Alex, then back to the woman who was most likely his girlfriend. "This guy bothering you?" He flipped a thumb in Alex's direction.

"He's been staring," she said as she cupped her hands under her breasts and gave them a substantial boost.

"Wow," Alex said to no one in particular. Half his blood remained in his face while the other half pooled into the tight quarters of his crotch.

The man got out of the booth and stood over Alex. "Punk-ass little pervert," he said. "Take a seat somewhere else."

"I won't look anymore," Alex said. "I swear."

"Not good enough." The man picked up the little dish of peach cobbler from Alex's tray and plunked it onto his nose.

The cobbler was like molten lava. Alex let out a horrified moan. Then he saw Lester in his periphery.

"What the hell's going on?" Lester said to the man.

Alex began wiping the gooey mess off his face.

"This pervert's been harassing my girl."

"He did no such thing," Lester said. "And he's not a pervert."

"Listen, Old Timer, this is none of your business."

"When you assault my friend, I make it my business." Lester raised his stick with both hands and lowered his stance as if preparing for an outside fastball. The entire dining room fell silent. A few people were standing. "Back off right now," he continued, "or I'll pop your head into next week."

The boyfriend didn't budge. He looked down at Alex and gave him a little swat on the forehead. "You're a prize," he said, "a pervert and a nigger lover."

The whole crowd seemed to gasp in unison.

Lester's face had turned monstrous. Sparks could have charged out of his eyeballs. He swirled the stick one revolution and swung.

Whack!

Some foul utterance came out of the boyfriend's mouth. He raised his hands to the side of his face and crouched to the floor. Blood trickled over his fingers and onto his watch. The girlfriend knelt beside him and tried to put her arms around his chest. But he pushed her out of the way and rose to his feet. For one brief moment, he lowered his hands. There was a bloody gash from his left cheek to the top of his ear. He stared at Lester and said, "I'm not through with you." Then he marched out of the restaurant, his girlfriend running after him.

The crowd of patrons erupted into gasps and chatter. There was light applause for Lester, and there was even one little man who laughed. A skinny waitress with bad complexion rushed to the table with Styrofoam boxes and a plastic bag. "Here," she said, "I'll pack up your food. Y'all should get out of here." Her Southern twang carried a sense of urgency. She peered out at the parking lot. "Looks like he's gone, but no telling when he'll be back. There'll be no charge for the food."

She began dumping the contents of the plates into containers, paying no mind to the laws of food separation.

"I think she's right," Alex said. He dabbed his face with a wet napkin to clear away the last of the stickiness.

Lester leaned against a chair. His eyes were closed. The air went in and out of him like a gated rodeo bull, but he just stood there. And then he nodded, grabbed his stick and began walking. Alex followed closely behind trying to remember a time when someone had stood up for him the way Lester had. It didn't take a lot of searching. There was no one. The realization made him want to cry.

The day was sweltering, far too bright, and there were swarms of gnats like microscopic piranha chomping at his scalp. He brushed them off with his free hand while carrying the food with the other, all the while scanning the parking lot for muscle-bound racists. If he saw the bloody boyfriend again, he was perfectly willing to smack the cartons of food at him then run like hell. Not exactly bravery, but it was a plan.

But the man was either gone, tending his wound, or he was well-concealed between vehicles. That made sense if he wanted to identify Lester's car.

At the Cadillac, Lester pulled the keys out of his pocket and said, "You're behind the wheel, kid." He lowered himself into the passenger seat.

Alex got in and started the engine. He adjusted the air conditioner to full blast. Then he looked over and said, "You okay?"

Lester nodded and said, "You just worry about driving."

"What about the food?"

"We'll eat after we cross the Florida line. It's not far." He had raised his hands to his eyes and was now looking at them like they'd betrayed him.

"You sure you're okay?"

"Hit that son of a bitch harder than I expected."

"Maybe the stick wasn't such a good idea after all."

"I'm not sorry I hit him. I just hope he doesn't come full of testosterone and hunt us down."

"Me too," Alex said.

"Every man's got a streak of anger inside him. If a man says he doesn't, he's either lying or castrated. Sometimes there's no telling how or when the anger'll come."

"You talking about him or you?"

"Both," Lester said, "mostly me. I've been angry since the day I was born."

"Why's that?"

"It's not a story you ought to hear," he said. Then he closed his eyes and went silent.

CHAPTER ELEVEN

As they approached the state of Florida, Alex expected an oversized billboard jammed with a collage of alligators, oranges, pastel beaches and Mickey Mouse, all bordering a space shuttle at mid-launch. But the actual sign was generic blue, no bigger than a movie poster.

Lester pointed to an exit ramp and directed Alex to a shady spot behind a gas station. A cluster of cigarette butts surrounded a couple of inverted five-gallon buckets that would do for seating.

Alex sat across from Lester and ate while listening to the old man complain about how his roast beef was covered with dressing and mixed in with his salad. He said everything was the same temperature. Then, after a few more bites, he said, "I've had all I can stomach." He got up and tossed the rest of his food into a nearby dumpster.

Alex kept eating while watching Lester. The old man opened the door behind the passenger seat and pulled out his stick. He held it under brilliant sunlight and spun it around slowly. Then he went back to the trunk and searched around. He pulled out a first aid kit and found an alcohol prep pad, using it to rub the end of the stick. Afterward, he slammed the trunk and said, "No more racist blood on my stick."

Alex offered a nervous smile.

Buckled up and in the passenger seat Lester said, "For better or worse, I believe I'm developing a fondness for that stick."

THEY WERE back on the road, traveling through the heart of Jacksonville but with very little traffic. Both remained silent for a long time while the tension in Alex's chest expanded. He wasn't afraid of the old man going psycho, whacking away with his stick. But he was worried about Lester's health if he kept having outbursts. The other thing Alex didn't like was being censored out of Lester's history. After thirty or so minutes, he couldn't take it any longer. "I'm not a little kid, you know."

Lester shook his head slowly. "It's not a pleasant story."

"Fine with me," Alex said. "Pleasant stories are boring."

Lester smiled and said, "All right, but first you gotta realize, I'm not blaming anybody here, not even myself. It's just the way things were."

Alex nodded.

"You see, my mother had this thing. She called it a weekly purification before the Lord's Day. Nowadays, you'd call it abuse. Every Saturday she beat the snot out of me and my brother and my three sisters. Went on every week till I turned twelve."

"Sounds worse than my mother."

"But the thing is, after I turned twelve, she stopped. And I had a lot to do with it." The old man's breathing seemed to catch. Alex didn't say anything.

"I snapped," Lester said. "But it wasn't out of nowhere. I saw my brother and sisters get beaten the same way every week. I took it too. I kept thinking my father would step in and put an end to it."

"Why didn't he?"

Lester raised a finger to hush Alex. "It was my twelfth birthday. My father asked me the day before what I wanted for a present. I said I wanted momma to stop beating us. He didn't say anything. But I thought, maybe."

There was a lengthy pause. Then Lester said, "Next day was Saturday. Momma lined us up just like she always did. And Papa sat on the front porch drinking, just like he always did. When it came my turn to take a beating, I was way too jacked up."

Another pause. "What did you do?"

"Best I remember, when momma raised her arm with that switch drawn back, I pounced. Grabbed her arm and twisted her to the floor. Then I bent her arm back and snapped it. Broke it in two places."

"Holy shit!" Alex said.

"I was just as mad at my father as I was at her. And when he stormed in from the porch, I gave him the meanest look I could muster. He just looked down at both of us. Didn't say a goddamn word. My father, you see; he was no idiot. But he had no earthly idea what to do."

"You must've gotten into some serious trouble."

"I'm sure I did, but that was small compared to what I got."

"What do you mean?"

"I got her to stop the beatings. And I got my self-respect. On that day I learned that you've got to stand up for yourself in this world, or you just keep taking beatings."

"You made up with her?"

"That's the strangest of it all," Lester said. "She was actually good to me after that...good as she could be." He went on to describe his siblings, how they were all intelligent, but Lester was the only one who had made something of himself. His older brother, Earl Jr., turned into an even bigger drunk than his father. His sister Mary—a straight-A student through high school—went crazy and lived a good chunk of her life in a state institution. Another sister, Esther, gave birth to one baby after another, barely raising any of them. Earlene was the only sibling still alive, and she had turned into an obese hermit.

"I was the one who made my mother proud," Lester said. "I graduated *magna cum laude* at Tuskegee with a degree in engineering. I worked for one of the most powerful companies in the world, made enough money to buy the house she'd been renting, buy her a car and much more."

Alex grinned and said, "So the moral of the story is to beat the shit out of your mother if you want to get ahead in life. I just might be able to do that."

"See I knew you'd miss the point."

"I'm only kidding," Alex said. "So how come you never got married or had kids?"

"One story at a time."

"So you'll tell me later?"

"Don't know." He paused and stared at Alex. "But I will say this. You ought to be more discreet when you're checking out a woman's equipment."

ALEX HAD driven over three straight hours without a break. The dashboard clock read twenty minutes to ten. The old man lay sleeping on the backseat, apparently unconcerned about the risk of getting ticketed for not having his seatbelt on or, if they hit anything, becoming a projectile. Alex had to suppress images of the car slamming into a wayward vehicle, catapulting Lester's body onto the hood.

He looked back to check if the old man was okay. His arm was draped behind him like he was playing a game of *guess which hand?* And his sleeping face, which had looked so angry at the truck stop, was the slumbering image of peace.

Finally, Lester made a series of dramatic sighs as he worked his way up to vertical. "Where are we?" he asked groggily.

"Commercial Boulevard is four miles."

"Good. That's our exit."

As if Alex didn't know. On Commercial, he would head east three-and-a-half miles and cross a drawbridge into Lauderdale-by-the-Sea. Then he'd go south a mile on A1A, take a left, and he'd be staring at his father's high-rise condo. He had spent hour after hour studying the map, visualizing the building, the palm trees and the white-capped waves. He was almost there.

They drove a few blocks down A1A in search of a decent-looking place to stay. It was too late to be choosey. Lester pointed to a little one-story motel with the word vacancy lit up in green. Just above was the motel name, Palm Grotto.

Alex squeezed the Cadillac into the alley behind the motel and angled into the first open spot. He got out and leaned against the trunk while Lester made arrangements in the office. In just a few minutes the old man came out and said, "Place is practically empty. We'll see if the room isn't too bad." He handed Alex a key with the number 8 embossed in a plastic diamond. "Don't lose this, or it costs me fifty bucks."

Alex nodded. "I'll get the bags."

The room was floral everything—not the French Impressionist

floral but the Michael's Crafts variety. A plastic daisy arrangement sprung out of a plastic vase. There was gardenia wallpaper and vine-striped bedspreads on two double beds. But no palms and no grottos, except for the inadequate lighting, which felt a bit cave-like. Alex decided he didn't want to lie next to the air conditioner rattling all night long, so he set his own bag on the bed farthest from the window, hoisting Lester's suitcase onto the dresser.

"Guess this room'll make us appreciate our feminine side," Lester said as he set his shaving kit onto the vanity. "Least it's clean."

Alex sat at the edge of his bed lost in pleasant thoughts. This trip was starting to feel like destiny in the making. Even these small details—this room, Lester's shaving kit, the stick against the dresser. They all felt as if they belonged. Less than a mile down the road was his father. What an amazing concept!

Lester came out of the bathroom dressed in the same pin-striped pajamas. He shuffled his way to the bed by the window and pulled back a corner of covers.

"Thanks for doing this," Alex said.

Lester stood still for a moment. "I'm glad to be here."

THE MOST frustrating aspect of traveling with Lester was the slowness of his gaitv, stick or no stick. Even though the pier was just a few blocks away, they had to stop five times for the old man to catch his breath. Alex tried not to let his impatience show, but when they finally arrived at the beach, he marched down through freckled sand while Lester sat on a bench by the parking lot.

Alex felt the need to shed something of his old self, and the ocean water was the perfect place to do it. He studied the gentle waves and the sea stretching out to meet the curved horizon. The early morning sun was already a good distance above the ocean, almost directly in front of him. The breeze was warm, with a choppy thickness, and it carried the odor of gutted fish from the pier. Overweight seagulls fought over a piece of bread while a pelican flew reconnaissance just offshore. There was a yacht of some significance made small by its far-off distance. Farther out were a couple of cargo ships dwarfed to the size of the capsules Alex was supposed to be taking. He narrowed his eyes and tried to determine which way the ships were traveling.

Then he reached into his mouth, and he threw the shiny object as far as he could into the sunlight.

THE FIRST section of the pier was a restaurant where Alex and Lester would have breakfast. They sat across from each other in a wooden booth with minimal padding. Lester faced east, toward the ocean while Alex had a view of the parking lot.

"It's a big day," Lester said, opening his menu. "You nervous?"

"No," Alex said then caught himself. "Well, maybe a little."

"You ought to call him before you show up at his door. Most people don't like to be shocked."

"If I call, he might find a way to back out."

Lester nodded sternly. "Good point."

A waitress arrived to take their order.

"I'll have coffee," Lester said, "two eggs scrambled, grits and rye toast, plenty of butter."

She took his menu.

"A bowl of Frosted Flakes," Alex said, "large orange juice and a cherry danish."

Lester grimaced. "If I ate like that, you'd have to book me a slot at the local morgue."

Legitimate point, Alex thought but didn't say anything. The waitress smiled then turned away.

"So you want to surprise him then," Lester said.

"I'm hoping he won't mind."

"He probably will. You should be ready for that."

"I am," Alex said. "Anything's better than being ignored." He opened his mouth wide, displaying the empty spot in place of the silver knob.

"You got rid of it."

"Yup, just a few minutes ago."

"You're done pissing off your mother?"

"For now, I guess."

"Think your father'll like you better without that damn thing in your tongue?"

"No, I don't care. That's not why I did it." But when he thought about it a little further, he realized the old man was right.

"When do you want to see him?"

"Right after breakfast."

DRIVING SOUTH on A1A, Alex recognized the sequence of intersections to his father's building. The route was cleaner than he had expected. The buildings were taller, palm trees more abundant and the grass thicker than the pictures of his mind. The other thing about the grass was that it was cut flush against the curb, giving it a look of refinement. He was starting to like his new surroundings.

And then, there it was—twenty-eight stories high—the Galt Atlantic.

He pressed the left blinker and turned toward the parking garage, which lay below the residential part of the building. A booth with a gate operator kept them from going any further. Alex's chest felt like it was seizing up on him.

A black man in a security uniform slid open his window. "Who you visiting?"

Alex wasn't sure he'd be able to speak. "Uh," he said. "Scott Riley, twelve-twenty-four." His voice was definitely quivering. "I'm his son, Alex."

The man looked beyond Alex and nodded at Lester. "I'll still need to check." He closed his window and picked up a phone. Then he started talking, but Alex couldn't read his lips.

"Looks like somebody's up there," Lester said.

The guard peered at Alex and nodded. The gate went up.

"Wow," Alex said. "He's letting us in."

"It's a good start."

CHAPTER TWELVE

It felt like Lester was taking the whole morning as he made his grueling way to the elevator. Slouched against the doorframe, Alex waited nervously. *Come on, old man,* he wanted to say. But he just stood there staring at the big orange G painted on the concrete wall. He guessed it stood for *Ground*, or perhaps *Garage*. Interchangeable G's, he thought, and it made him feel good to know that his brain still worked.

Lester repeated his mantra, "Patience, kid," as he poked his way with his stick and entered the elevator. Alex pushed the number twelve and stepped back. The door closed, but the elevator stopped one flight up at a marbled lobby, picking up a couple of old ladies in bathing suits and towels. They got off at the fourth. Alex and Lester had the elevator to themselves up to twelve.

"Guess you know what you're planning to say," Lester said.

It was sort of true. In fact, Alex had practiced and modified his opening line many times over the past year. He wasn't about to rehash it in the elevator with Lester. "I've got it pretty well down," was all he said. He was starting to wonder how he'd explain Lester's presence. It was probably best to tell his father the truth. Lying was for parents you already knew.

Alex held the door while Lester stepped through. The hallway was long and carpeted maroon. Conical lights were spaced about every fifteen feet. Each door had a peephole and a series of silver numbers. Between huffs and puffs Lester said, "It's one hell of an elegant place."

Alex's mind barely registered the remark. He walked five paces in front of Lester and stopped at the end of the hall. To his right was a door with the numbers 1224. His stomach was like a fisherman's knot. He took a couple of deep breaths and waited. The hallway was probably set at a reasonable temperature, but it was a meat locker to Alex.

"Go ahead," Lester said. "Whenever you're ready."

Alex pressed the button and heard a series of bells on the other side.

There was the muffled sound of a man's voice, then a woman's. Someone was coming.

Alex cleared his throat.

The door swung halfway open. "Alex," his mother said, "what a relief."

"Well, I'll be damned," Lester said.

"You two have no idea how much trouble you've caused."

"What the hell!" Alex said. "What are you doing here?"

His mother was wearing a silk robe covering a one-piece bathing suit. "I came here to find you," she said. "I knew where you were going."

"Where is he?" Alex asked.

"Your father's at his restaurant. He's agreed to see you there before we leave."

"Bullshit," Alex said. "I leave when I'm ready." He took a step forward. Anger seemed to counteract his nerves. "I heard a man in here."

"That would be Bill," his mother said. Then she called out, "BILL."

Alex stood in the center of a circular vestibule. Beyond, he could see a living room filled with red leather furniture and two glass walls converging at a mighty column. The windowed wall to his left overlooked the Atlantic Ocean. The view directly ahead was another high rise. Lester came up from behind and patted Alex's shoulder.

A faucet, which had been running, shut off. Bill stepped into the living room wearing nothing but a royal blue Speedo bathing suit. His hairless torso was milky and sunburn pink. The roll of flesh hanging over his waistband was pocked and webbed with stretch marks. "Hello, Alex, Mr. Bray," Bill said, "good to see you." He extended a hand.

Neither of them took it.

"Holy shit," Alex said. "Everything's getting weirder and weirder."

Alex's mother touched his arm, but he thrust it back. "Don't touch me," he said, backing away.

"Listen, Alex," she said, "I'm making arrangements for you to fly back with us tomorrow." She turned to face Lester. "And Mr. Bray, I'm sorry but you'll have to drive yourself back up or get someone else to go with you. Furthermore, I don't appreciate what you've done."

Lester nodded. "I don't imagine you do, ma'am."

"Don't listen to her," Alex said, turning to his mother. "You can't make me go with you. I leave with Lester when we're both ready." He wished the old man's hand was still on his shoulder.

"We'll talk about it later." His mother tightened her robe. "I'm getting dressed. Then I'll take you to see your father. Mr. Bray, feel free to use the phone to make arrangements for yourself." She turned abruptly toward the hallway.

Bill remained in the living room. He looked like he didn't know what to do with his hands. "Think I'll go change too," he said.

"Fabulous idea," Lester said then smiled at Alex. "Come on, kid, cheer up. Everything's gonna work out the way it's supposed to." He made his way over to the ocean view and replanted the stick in front of him. He looked like a dilapidated tripod.

Alex stepped forward without saying anything.

"Now ain't this something?" Lester said.

Alex tried to appreciate the view, but his mind was too wrapped up. "Don't worry," he said, almost whispering. "I'm not getting on any plane with them."

Lester turned his head toward Alex. "We'll see what you do."

ALEX AND his mother walked a good distance apart from each other in the parking garage before converging at a red convertible Mustang. She pressed a button, and the car chirped. "Nice car," Alex said. "Is it dad's?"

"It's our rental." Then she smiled. "It is nice, though. I'm putting the top down."

"I can drive, you know. I've done it most of the way down here." The declaration was almost true. Just under half, he figured.

"I assumed Mr. Bray didn't drive the whole way down by himself. I hope he taught you well." She got into the driver's seat and turned the ignition.

"Let me drive this thing," Alex said, still standing. "I'll show you myself."

"You're not driving this car!" Her words came out like ballistics.

"Easy, mom." He waited for the top to disappear before getting in.

"Well, you're not insured to drive it." She backed out of the spot and turned toward the exit ramp. The engine was a symphony of muscle echoing off the walls and ceiling and back into Alex's ribcage, which was starting to tremor all over again. He was finally going to see his father.

Free of the garage, they went south on A1A passing more condos, a few hotels, boutique shops, an ice cream parlor and fancy houses with walls around them. Then, on the left side, the road opened to the beach and the sun-streaked ocean.

The alarming brightness of it all forced him to shade his eyes with his hand. He could see an elaborate lifeguard structure made of fiberglass and aluminum legs. If someone stamped on the NASA logo, it could have passed for a lunar module. The day was good for sunbathers, and there were quite a few—mostly older people who probably should have been more concerned with calories than pigmentation.

A couple more traffic signals and they turned right. A quick left and they were in the parking lot of The Flaming Coral.

Alex remained in his seat.

"I'm perfectly willing to go in with you," his mother said, turning off the engine.

"I'm doing this myself."

His mother was wearing the kind of sunglasses that mirrored your stretched out face. "Before you go in," she said, "there's something I want you to know."

"What's that?"

"I don't suppose it matters to you. In fact, I'm sure it doesn't. But I loved your father very much. That's how it was. I loved him."

"Is that all?"

She didn't say anything. It seemed like she was about to cry, in which case Alex couldn't get out of the car quickly enough. "I'm going in," he said. "You stay away."

The door to the restaurant was a mass of solid teak with a urethane-coated rope to pull it open. He stared at the rope. Suddenly his opening line no longer felt right. Who the hell walks up to somebody in a restaurant and says, "I've been waiting fifteen years to meet you?" It felt hollow and pathetic.

His chest pounded as he gripped the rope. He had no idea what to say. One glance back at his mother in the Mustang. Her seat was reclined, and she had taken off her shades to keep from getting raccoon eyes. She was basking in the rays and moving her head to some awful Barry Manilow song.

He opened the door and stepped inside. The place was divided, equal parts bar to the left and restaurant to the right, but Alex's eyes were naturally drawn upward to the luminescent coral spanning much of the vaulted ceiling. It glowed with a stunning variety of hues. And even though it was probably plastic, it pulsated with life—each branch changing color before him. The effect was magical.

"First time here?" It was a cheerful man's voice directly in front of him.

"Yeah." Alex lowered his head. "It is."

"Well, if you're here for the bar, I'll have to card ya." He gave an exaggerated frown. "Or I can seat you in the restaurant. We have some wonderful specials."

"No, actually I'm here to see my father." God, he was nervous. "I mean, my dad." What the hell difference did it make?

"Hmm," the man said, "that's a new one." He was wearing a V-neck T that hugged him like another layer of skin. "You sure you're in the right place?"

"His name's Scott Riley."

The man's head snapped back, and his cheerful demeanor turned to shock. "You're joking."

"I haven't seen him in a long time. He won't recognize me."

"Well, I'll be a monkey's uncle." The man pointed to the bar. "Look that way."

Alex turned to face the bar. He could feel the man's stare. Could this be him?

"Come to think of it, you do have his chin." He held Alex by the jaw to keep it from moving. "Same nose too. I'll take you to see him myself. My name's Roger."

Alex followed past the curvilinear bar. There were only a few people sitting at it and a couple of men standing at a cocktail table. They nodded at him.

Alex nodded back. Friendly place.

"Right back here," Roger said.

They entered a kitchen with a loud fan. A guy with a ponytail was stirring something in a huge cast iron pot. The smell was otherworldly, like something from Bangkok or maybe Bangladesh. Alex tried to picture a man with a chin and cheekbones like his.

They approached a glossy red door at the rear of the building, near the exit. "He should be here," Roger said, knocking on the door.

"Come in," said a man's voice.

Roger opened the door about a foot and stuck his head in. "I've got a guy here who says he's your son."

Some words passed back and forth, but all Alex could hear was the industrial fan. Roger pulled his head from the door and looked at Alex. "You can go in." His voice had lost its bounce.

The will to step into the room was unconscious. Alex felt nothing but the pounding of his chest. His body commanded itself forward— four cloudlike steps to the center of a rectangular office. His eyes tracked the man in front of him.

"Alex," the man said. "It's really you." He rose from his desk and stepped closer. His eyes were moist. His hands went to the outsides of Alex's shoulders and settled there.

"Yeah it's me," Alex said, reminding himself to breathe. "I came a long way."

"I know," his father said. "I think it's awesome."

Alex searched for a chord of resemblance. The man's skin was smooth and tan. His hair was short, almost crew-cut length, and he wore a neatly groomed mustache and beard. He had a silver earring in his left ear shaped like a martini glass with a little green gem for an olive. "I saw your apartment," Alex said. "It's nice. So is this place."

"We've done quite well." He lowered his hands. "I should get you something to eat." He was standing eye-to-eye with Alex. The two were exactly the same height.

"I'm not hungry," Alex said, "but I'll take a soda."

"Sure, what kind do you like?"

"Dr. Pepper."

His father nodded. "I used to like that too." He stuck his head out the door and called after someone to bring the soda. Then he shut the door and said, "Closest thing we have is Cherry Coke. Have a seat."

Alex would have preferred standing, but he didn't want to make a defiant first impression. So he lowered himself into a round chair that swiveled.

"I had a feeling I'd see you," his father said, "before your mother called."

"I don't want to talk about her. She ruins everything."

"Can't disagree with you there. But I'll bet she's done a fine job raising you."

That was debatable, but Alex didn't say anything. He hadn't come here to say nice things about his mother.

Someone knocked on the door. His father opened it just enough so that the soup-stirring man with the ponytail could stick in his head and get a good look. "I see the resemblance," the man said, "a vast improvement over the original." He handed the can of soda to Alex's father but kept looking at Alex. "Want a glass with ice?"

"No," Alex said, "as long as it's cold." He could feel his nerves settle as he snapped open the can and took a swig. The door was closed again.

His father sat on top of the desk. "You came all this way on your own?" He crossed his legs.

"No, I came with a friend." He was getting a little annoyed. His father must have known about Lester.

"That's right, your mother mentioned an elderly man."

"His name's Lester," Alex said. "He's a good man."

"Do you have a girlfriend?"

"I'm working on it. There's this girl named Britney. She's on the cross-country team."

"Britney," said his father. "Bet she's pretty."

"Yeah," Alex said. "But I don't think she's interested." He didn't want to talk about Britney, fearing it might jinx his prospects.

"How've you been doing in school?"

He definitely didn't want to talk about school. "Fine," he said then took another sip from the can. "A's in everything but gym."

"That's excellent." His father smiled broadly, the same kind of smile Alex had dreamt about. But, oddly, it didn't have much effect. It was like a cop out. Sure, it was easy to show paternal pride now. Far too easy. And trivial, like it meant nothing. Maybe that was the problem. After all the waiting and all the build-up, anything they talked about would probably seem trivial. They might as well talk about the tropical breeze coming off the ocean and then call it a day.

After a marked pause in conversation, it occurred to Alex that the only thing worth talking about was his father's absence. Fifteen years of nothing. How would he explain that?

"I can tell that you're angry," his father said. "You can admit it."

It was unnerving that the man could tell what Alex was feeling. "I'm not angry." It was his first lie to his father.

"It's your nostrils. I do the same thing." His father scrunched his face and flared his nostrils. Quite a menacing look. "Go ahead, Alex, say what you want to say."

Alex was stuck on the idea that someone could read his face. He looked down at the dark space between the stone floor and the desk. Then the words just leaped out: "How come you never tried to contact me?"

"That's not true." His father uncrossed his legs. "I've been writing you ever since I left. Last time was a little over a week ago for your sixteenth birthday, along with a check."

Totally ridiculous, Alex thought, the boldest lie he'd ever heard.

But then a long familiar image flashed before him. It was the locked mailbox on his front porch. His mother had said it was there to keep undesirables from stealing her identity and her magazines. His anger was changing vector. "I got some money deposited into my college fund," he said, making a fist of his free hand. "But I never got a letter from you...ever."

His father shook his head, nostrils flaring. He might have been acting, in which case he missed his true calling. "Where is she?" He spoke the words slowly.

"Out in her rental car," Alex said. "I can get her to come in."

"No." His father held up a hand. "Like you said, she ruins everything. I don't want her ruining our first time together. I'll deal with her later."

"You wrote me a lot?"

"I did," his father said. "Nearly once a month for the past fifteen years." He looked up toward his left, giving him a look of computation. "Must be about 150 letters. Some were long. Some were barely anything. I tried to account for your age when I wrote them, and I figured at some point you'd write me back. Guess now I know why that hasn't happened."

"That's so messed up," Alex said. "She keeps a lock on our mailbox. I always thought it was to keep her mail and her identity from being stolen."

His father's nostrils were still at it. "Your mother's a hell of a piece of work. Unbelievable."

"So I missed a lot of stuff?"

"You missed everything, son."

It was the word he'd been waiting to hear. Son. He was part of the universe of boys who had fathers. It made him feel like crying. He'd have to change the subject.

There were a lot more questions to ask. He stared at the can of soda. "How come you never called or came up for a visit?"

"There's no good answer for that," his father said. "I've thought about it more than you can imagine. Only excuse I have is shame. And I know that's not good enough." His shoulders were slumping. "Letter-writing just felt more comfortable, more permanent. I wanted you to compile a record of your wayward father."

"Yeah," Alex said, "but you never got to hear about me."

"I know," his father said. "This isn't meant as an excuse, Alex, but let me back up to when your mother and I first separated. You probably know that I was the one who wanted out. She was understandably hurt and angry. So she hired this Neanderthal lawyer to rake me over. The guy had the family court judge in his back pocket."

Alex pictured a scene of his mother's high-profile cronies in black suits throwing their weight around.

"I ended up having to pay five grand a month, and all I got was an hour a week with you—supervised, no less. And your mother had final say over who the supervisor was. She chose her father...who, of course, hated me."

Alex's grandfather was long dead, so it wouldn't be easy to verify that claim.

"I endured about nine or ten of those visits under the man's watchful eyes and constant criticism. It felt like I was taking a beating every time." He threw his hands into the air. "So I left. I stopped trying to see you." His voice started to crack. "I wish I would've handled it differently." A couple of tears streaked down his face and onto his white Oxford shirt.

Things had reversed themselves. Now Alex wanted to cry, but somehow he couldn't. "It's okay now," he said. "It's over."

Another knock at the door.

His father didn't bother to wipe his eyes. "Come in."

The ponytailed man stuck his head in. "Sorry to interrupt, but we've got twelve orders up."

"I'll be right there," his father said. "Give us another minute."

When the door closed, he stood in front of Alex and said, "Come here, son. I want to give you a hug...if you'll let me."

That's when it happened. That's when Alex broke down and cried. He set his Cherry Coke on the desk and put his arms around his father.

When they separated, his father said, "Your mother made plans for all of us to have breakfast tomorrow at my place. I'm changing that plan. Your mother and Bill won't be invited. But I want you to come, and please bring your friend." He jotted down his cell number on the back of a multi-colored business card.

Alex slipped the card into his wallet. He retrieved his half-empty soda, hugged his father one last time, and then he walked out the back door.

CHAPTER THIRTEEN

Outside, he passed a shaded picnic table where a man in a straw hat held a pipe to his mouth. Alex wondered how bad his face looked from all the tears. He un-tucked his shirt and wiped his eyes while walking around to the front of the building.

The red Mustang was still blaring crappy music—Hall and Oats, no less. His mother was all the way reclined. Her eyes were still shut, but her head wasn't moving anymore. She was probably asleep. He held the can of Cherry Coke above her and poured the rest of it onto her face.

She bolted upright. "What the hell's gotten into you?" She shook her head like a dog after a bath.

"You're the one to talk," he said. "Stealing my mail from dad!" He ricocheted the empty can off the Mustang's hood. "That's a new low."

"Get in the car," she said, turning off the radio. "I can explain."

"Bullshit. You'll never be able to explain that." He began walking toward A1A, crossing over to the beach side of the highway.

His mother pulled up alongside and began shouting for his attention. He extended a middle finger and then placed the tips of his fingers into his ears. The last thing he heard her say was, "I did it to protect you."

Cars behind her were honking. Finally, his mother sped off.

And then, for no good reason, Alex began jogging.

When that wasn't enough, he charged into a full-throttled sprint. It was the second time in a week that he had broken into a run. He could run for miles. That's how good it felt.

BUT HIS underworked lungs couldn't take it for very long. He slowed to a walk, then stopped at a bench shaded by palm trees. It might have been the run or the thoughts darting in and out of his brain, or maybe it was the scorching mid-day sun that had wiped him out so much. He lay on the slats of wood and closed his eyes.

When he woke up, the shade was no longer coming from the palm trees but from the two-story building across the divided street. He looked at his watch. It was 6:30. He had slept for over two hours, and he was starving. But the bigger concern was Lester.

Alex walked toward the motel, which was right on A1A, so it was easy to find. Lester wasn't in the room, but he'd left a note on the first bed. It was written on Palm Grotto stationary. It said:

I borrowed a pair of your shorts. I'm at the beach by the pier.
Meet me.

Alex didn't feel like swimming, but he grabbed a towel from the bathroom in case Lester had forgotten to bring his own. There was a little sign over the toilet strictly forbidding guests from bringing towels to the beach. Alex stuffed the towel under his shirt and began walking.

Once he arrived at the beach, finding Lester was simple. Fifteen feet from water's edge, the stick was pointing nearly vertical. Another thirty feet out in the water, and there stood Lester. He raised an arm. Alex waved back. He still didn't want to swim, but he was willing to get his feet wet. He took off his sneakers and headed for the water.

He watched as Lester pushed slowly toward the shore with a look of strain on his face. Alex remembered from physics that every wave, regardless of how small, drew back an opposing force beneath it. Plus the old man was essentially walking uphill, which meant that the problem of leaving the water was greater than that of getting in. His frame was arched forward as he cupped his hands against the surf.

Alex flashed back to Lester's angina attack at the truck stop. Down here at the beach, there would be no nitro tablets to the rescue. He ran back to dry sand, grabbed the stick and headed toward Lester. "Hold on," he yelled. The water was past his kneecaps. "I'll pull you in."

Lester didn't say anything. He was probably too winded to speak. He reached for the stick with one hand then the other.

"Just stay on your feet," Alex said.

Once they were clear of the water, Lester dropped to a knee.

Alex handed him the stick. "Here, hold onto it."

Gradually Lester's breathing slowed out of the urgent care range. He used the stick to rise to his feet. Then, finally, he spoke. "Glad you were here. Otherwise I'd have to wait for a tugboat."

Alex smiled, feeling proud of the accomplishment.

"I don't plan on dying right away," Lester continued. "But when I do, I want you to put this stick in the casket with me." He squeezed it with both hands. "That's what I'd like you to do."

Alex began brushing the sand off his feet so that he could put his socks and shoes back on. "That's not gonna be for a long time."

Lester was now facing the ocean, stick propped in front of him. "We'll see."

"You sorry you went in?"

"Not at all. It was great, made me feel totally refreshed."

"That's good," Alex said. "I'm glad."

"While you were out, I found a bank with a notary. It's official: the Caddy's yours when I pass."

"Can't we talk about something other than death?"

"Pick a subject," Lester said, "any subject."

"I should tell you how it went with my dad."

"I'd like to hear it. I already know how it went with your mother. You can skip that part."

"You saw her?"

"She came back to the condo like a deranged animal. Told me how you walked off after pouring soda on her face."

"She tell you why?"

"She did," Lester said. "I became her makeshift confessional. She told about the letters your father wrote and that ridiculous mailbox."

"She's a flat-out deceitful bitch."

"True enough," Lester said. "She'd stop at nothing to keep you from knowing the truth. By the way, I'm supposed to tell you to call her."

Alex felt as if a bug had stung his forehead then flown away. "Keep me from knowing what truth?"

"You know, kid, that your father's gay."

"That's bullshit. He can't be gay."

"Why not?"

"You're crazy," Alex said. "There's no way."

"But it's true," Lester said. "Sorry you had to hear it from me."

"My dad's not gay!"

"Suit yourself." Lester pulled his stick out of the sand and started collecting his clothes.

"Fuck you," Alex said. "You never met him." He started walking away, toward the concrete struts supporting the pier. Then, briefly, he turned back and yelled, "And you never will!"

CHAPTER FOURTEEN

Alex maintained a southward course along the beach, not caring enough
to move away from the occasional surge of water spreading out in front
of him and lapping over his high-top sneakers, not caring when he
passed right by his father's condo without breaking his robotic stride.
The sun gradually gave way to a crescent moon above his left shoulder,
dark sky all around. How could his father be gay? The question formed
an endless loop, stranded in the no-man's-land of Alex's brain.

He kept walking. He could feel and hear the groaning of his
stomach. Last thing he ate was breakfast at the pier, over twelve hours
ago. He should find something to eat. But somehow suffering was
better. It was more appropriate.

In the spirit of further suffering, he veered left so that every
sloshing step kicked up a spray of water. It wasn't enough. He wanted
more pain, more suffering. He wanted to be closer to the source that
made everything rotten. So he charged into the water, plowing ahead
until the ocean floor under his shoes was no more. The night was
black. He lowered his head below the surface and screamed as loud as
his lungs could deliver.

His first screams were mindless babble. Then he shouted one string of obscenities after another—some above the waterline, most below the surface. Then he yelled, "Come eat me, you asshole sharks!" To punctuate his tirade, he flopped around like a toddler in a tub.

If he stayed like this, it wouldn't matter. Shark or no shark, he'd drown from pure exhaustion. To check the depth, he shot himself down like a pogo stick. It was at least twenty feet when his shoes finally struck bottom. Deeper than he'd expected. He propelled himself back up. When his head finally poked through the surface, he turned to face the brightly lit coastline. "No way!" He was nearly half a mile out.

He didn't want to die after all.

As he began swimming toward the shore, his mind flashed back to how feeble Lester had looked just a couple of hours earlier trying to make it to dry land. There was no comparison. Alex would not have to be dredged ashore by a stick. He was strong. But he would find a way to get stronger. If there was any lesson from his ocean scare, this was it. And by the time he made it to shallow water, the lesson became a promise. He would do whatever it took to get stronger.

But the ocean wasn't quite through with him. When he turned his head to suck air, a wave broke against his face causing him to snort saltwater. He hacked and coughed his way ashore. Kneeling on wet sand, he coughed until he was nearly crying.

"You okay?" It was a woman's scratchy voice.

He coughed a little more and said, "I'm fine." Then he stood up to see where the voice had come from.

The beach was a narrow ribbon of sand, no more than thirty feet from water to waist-high barrier wall. The woman was sitting on a concrete bench in an open section of wall where the sidewalk had expanded. To her left was a shopping cart. A blanket was spread across her lap and over the cart.

"Come here," she said. "Let me have a look at ya."

He couldn't think of a workable excuse, so he squished his way up the sand. The breeze felt cool against his wet clothing. "Hello," he said.

"Nice night for a swim?" Her face was big and round like a harvest moon, and her smile revealed gaps where there should have been teeth. As he got closer, he could see the scraggly beginnings of a beard.

"I guess so," he said, looking beyond to the road and the stretch of shops and bars and hotels. "I was just walking. I didn't think I'd go in."

"So you're impulsive," she said. "And you're nothing but skin and bones. Have a seat. I'll get you something to eat."

"You don't need to bother."

"Have a seat." She patted the empty side of bench then leaned the other way to her cart, pulling back the blanket. Alex sat at the edge of the bench, ready to spring if necessary. He angled himself to see what she was getting, fearing it might be dog food or a slice of discarded pizza.

"You're in luck," she said. "I've got the mother lode: Ding Dongs, Swiss Cake Rolls, Tostitos and Combos." She shoveled her hand through an elaborate pile of stuff. "What'll it be?"

"How'd you get all that?"

"These here are the nearly-expired. I get'em when the stores can't sell'em. They'd go to waste otherwise. You wouldn't believe all the things you can get for free just because of the date on the package."

"Are they safe to eat?"

"Course they are," she said. "They got preservatives. They're good as new." She pulled out a box with the face of Little Debbie and set it in the space between them. "Open up, help yourself."

He was beyond hungry. If the woman's hearing was even halfway decent, she could tell by the groans coming out of his stomach. He opened the box lid and pulled out a package of Swiss Cake Rolls. There were twelve, all unopened, ready to be devoured. He pulled apart the clear wrapping and stuffed an entire cake roll into his mouth.

It was good and sweet.

The woman was staring at him. "See what I'm saying?" The night breeze trailed past the woman and into Alex's nostrils, carrying the aroma of Log Cabin syrup mixed with sheets that hadn't been washed in a month.

"Yeah," he said, still chewing. "They're good."

"You live around here?"

"No, I'm from Albany, just outside of Albany, New York." He started on the second roll.

"We get a lot of you folks down here, mostly in winter." She reached inside her jacket. "You don't mind if I smoke, do ya?"

"No, go ahead," he said. Actually, he welcomed it—anything to cancel out the prevailing stench. She pulled out a cigarette, stuck it in her mouth and flicked a disposable lighter.

She inhaled and exhaled a couple of times then said, "What brings ya down?"

"My father lives here." He pointed to the box between them. "Mind if I have another?"

"Help yourself. I got vodka too. Would ya care for a taste?"

He wouldn't mind, even though he had never drunk vodka before. But he couldn't fathom putting his lips around the same bottle she drank from. Plus, he thought of his new pledge. "No thanks," he said, "I'm trying to get into shape."

"Well, those things won't help." She pointed to the snack roll going into his mouth.

"I oh," he mumbled, his mouth full. He'd have to pick up his efforts tomorrow.

"Your dad know your whereabouts?"

"I'm not staying with him."

"Who ya staying with, your girlfriend?" A vaguely familiar tune rang out of the woman's shopping cart.

"You got a cell phone?" he asked.

She pulled it out. "It's my daughter. She's the only one who calls, and I mean *only*." She flipped it open and brought it to her face. "Hi Joey."

Funny, Alex thought, everyone in the world had a cell phone but him. Even a homeless woman. He wondered if this put him into the category of the disenfranchised.

"I'm talking with a fine young man." She looked over at Alex and gave a little smile. He could do without her smile. "I'm fine, sweetie. Call ya later." She closed the phone.

"What was that song?" Alex asked. "Your ring-tone?"

"You recognize that one?"

"Sort of, but I can't place it."

"It's my all-time favorite: *Some Enchanted Evening* by Perry Como." She looked down at the phone as if Perry himself was there in miniature. "I can sing a bit of it if you like."

"No, that's okay."

"Really, I can sing it." She cleared her viscous throat and began, *Some enchanted evening...you may see a stranger...you may see a stranger...across an empty BEACH. And somehow you know...* She broke into hoarse laughter.

Alex smiled. "You did a change-up."

"Just for you, skinny."

"Mind if I use that phone?"

"You want to call your father?"

"No," Alex said, "my mother."

"Why, do I remind you of her?"

"Not one bit," Alex said. "And that's good for you."

She smiled her ghastly smile and handed him the phone.

He dialed his mother's cell. After two rings, he heard her say hello.

"It's me, mom."

"Hang on a second, Alex." There were people talking in the background. Then his mother said, "King, non-smoking, and a view of the ocean would be nice."

"Where are you?"

"We're checking in at the Howard Johnson's. Your father and I had a bit of a disagreement. You're staying here too, right?"

"Um...yeah," he said, wondering where she got that information. "I've got a question. Then I'm hanging up."

"Okay, Alex, what is it?"

"Is my father gay?"

There was a pause. Someone else was speaking to her. "Queen will be fine," she said. "I'm sorry, Alex."

"Answer the question, mom!"

"I thought you would've known by now," she said, "which shows how much you don't want to believe it. I didn't want to believe it either, trust me—"

He had heard enough. He closed the phone, passed it back to the woman and lowered his face into his hands.

She placed a hand on Alex's wet back and said, "That's a tough pill to swallow."

IT WAS just after midnight when Alex made his way back to the motel. He closed the door gently and kept the lights off so he wouldn't awaken Lester. The old man was smart. He had switched to the far bed, away from the clattering air conditioner.

Alex slipped into the first bed and tried to rid his mind of the day's craziness. It was probably three o'clock when sleep finally took over.

He woke to the sound of Lester in the shower. Then the damn telephone rang. It was probably a wake-up call meant for another room. He picked it up just to make it stop and left the receiver on the nightstand.

A tiny voice said, "Alex, I know you're there." It was his mother. How the hell had she found him? He sat up and stared at the phone. "Our plane leaves at 2:18. You'll have plenty of time for your brunch."

He thought of disguising his voice and telling her she had the wrong number. But there was an easier strategy. He hung up the phone.

One more stressful thing and his brain was liable to explode. Everything seemed to hit him at once, like a multiple-car pileup, or multiple boxers attacking the same heavy bag. He just sat on the bed, paralyzed, staring at the phone. The shower stopped. He pictured his mother and Bill tailing them to brunch then saying *Good luck* to Lester as they handed Alex his plane ticket. The old man would be left to fend for himself.

Forget brunch, he and Lester needed to get the hell out of there.

In a little while, Lester came out of the bathroom wearing nothing but a pair of wrinkled boxers. "Who called?" he asked.

"Wrong number."

"Missed you last night." There was no trace of anger in the old man's voice, which made Alex feel even guiltier about his verbal assault.

"I took a long walk and went in the ocean," Alex said. "It wasn't bad."

"Went in with your sneakers on?" He elbowed to the silhouetted sneakers perched on the windowsill while buttoning up a white shirt.

"Yeah, it was kind of impulsive."

"Guess it was," Lester said. "Your mom said something about breakfast at your dad's place. I can drop you off if you don't want me there."

"I'm not going," Alex said. "I don't want to be here anymore."

Lester had to sit halfway on the bed to put on his slacks. "Mind my asking why?"

"I should've believed you. And I shouldn't have said what I said."

"If that's an apology, then I accept."

"It is. I'm sorry I said that. I won't do it again."

"It's okay, kid." The old man zipped up and squared himself in front of Alex. "So what's next?"

"Any place but here." Alex rose from the bed. "Did you tell my mother where we're staying?"

"I told her the Howard Johnson's." Lester fed his belt through the loops. "I didn't want her calling all hours waking me up."

"Smart move," Alex said. He guessed that once his mother had discovered there was no Alex Riley or Lester Bray staying at the

Howard Johnson's, she and Bill frantically cruised up and down A1A checking motel parking lots. The old Caddy stuck out like one of those lunar modules on the beach.

"Take it you're not planning on getting on that plane," Lester said.

"Nope." Alex went over and grabbed his wet sneakers from the windowsill. His mother had probably seen them too.

"And you're not planning on staying down here with your father."

"Nope."

"So, what'll it be?"

"I thought we were going to see your sister in Alabama."

"That's what I thought too," Lester said. "But your mom being down here..." he let out a fatigued sigh. "She'll be one pissed-off broad by the time we're through with her."

"She'll get over it," Alex said. "It's not like her career's in jeopardy."

When they were both packed and ready, Lester walked into the bathroom and grabbed two hand towels. "These come with us," he said.

"Why?"

"I don't want anymore crumbs or greasy fingers touching my interior."

CHAPTER FIFTEEN

Alex drove while eating an egg sandwich. A towel lay across his lap to catch crumbs. His shoes remained wet and would probably reek by the time they reached their stopover. The speedometer held steady at seventy-two. He took a bite and focused on the flat stretch of turnpike, and he checked the rearview mirror. No red Mustang, thank God.

Driving had become enjoyable for Alex. He liked the feeling of progress, of relentless motion toward his objective. It hardly mattered that they were headed to some nowhere town to see an ancient woman he had no interest in meeting. What mattered was that he wasn't standing still. And he wasn't wallowing in the drama of his parents.

"What's the town like?" he asked to fill the silence.

"It's poor, and it's black," Lester said. "Blacker than you've ever seen."

"Why is that?"

"First, you gotta know about the region. It's the Bible Belt, the Black Belt and the Poor Belt all wrapped up into one."

Alex wanted to get it straight. "So the people are religious, black and poor."

"That's mostly how it is. You'll fit right in."

"You think that's funny?"

"Oh and there's football," Lester added. "We Alabamians love our football—worship it."

Alex hardly knew the difference between a line of scrimmage and a tight end. He made a silent pledge not to bring up the sport and expose himself as an idiot. But his greater concern was the Black Belt part of the equation. He pictured an army of black people with clubs and knives headed in his direction. "Is it tough for white people there?"

Lester wiped the last of his breakfast off his fingers. "If I'm not mistaken, you sound a bit scared."

"I'm not scared." It was a lie. "I just want to be prepared so I don't say anything stupid."

"Best thing you can do is be yourself. And put your racism aside."

"I'm not a racist," Alex said.

"Not in the strictest sense. But everyone carries some degree of racism. Think about it. You'll see what I mean."

Near Fort Pierce, the turnpike curved westward, away from the populated coastline. Alex kept his eyes on the highway and pondered the extent of his racism. Up until Lester, he had minimal contact with black people. There were probably eight or nine in his entire high school, and he couldn't recall exchanging more than a perfunctory greeting with any of them. His neighborhood was even whiter than his school. The only personal experiences he had with black people were when he was shopping or eating at restaurants. But for the sake of conversation he came up with something. "How come black people don't get out of the way on the sidewalk...or on the street?"

"Aha," Lester said. "That's your racism talking."

The idea made Alex cringe. His mother calling him a racist was one thing—ridiculous. Lester's accusation held some weight. "All right, so even if you're a tiny bit right, what am I supposed to do about it?"

"Understand it." The old man folded his towel and placed it in the center console. "I'll tell you something; I come from a race of people who've been oppressed for 350 years. You come from a 350-year line of oppressors. That's the difference between you and me."

"What does that have to do with standing in the middle of the street?"

"Well, kid, since I'm the only black person in the car," Lester glanced toward the backseat as if checking for stowaways, "I'll speak on behalf of the entire race. Here's what I think. I think it's about public spaces—streets and sidewalks, libraries and youth centers. We like to congregate, and we don't take that privilege lightly. Now that we've got our freedom to roam, we roam. We're out there doing our thing, walking our freedom walk."

"But it's rude to just stand there and block other people."

"I'd call it a small price. Step aside or wait. And while you're waiting, think about getting life from the shitty end of the stick."

LESTER PHONED his sister from a restaurant payphone near Ocala while Alex stood next to him in the shade of the red brick building. He was concerned about being a nuisance to Lester's sister, and he wondered if there'd be a spare bed for him. "Lunch was a bit of a wait," Lester said to his sister. "But we're making good time. Kid's a good driver." He gave a nod to Alex. Then he ended the conversation by saying, "See you tomorrow, sis. I expect mid-afternoon."

It was Lester's turn to drive. He adjusted the seat and mirrors and accelerated up the northbound ramp. "Figure we'll stop for the night in Valdosta, maybe further."

Alex unfolded the map and examined their route. "Tomorrow looks like an easy drive."

"More scenic too," Lester said. "We'll be getting off the interstate for good."

Alex put the map aside. He looked at Lester, straight ahead, then back toward Lester but didn't say anything.

"What's on your mind, kid? Cough it up."

"I'm just wondering," Alex said timidly. "Do you think being gay is a choice?"

"Ah," Lester said, "thinking about your father."

"Yeah, well I was just wondering."

"It's only my opinion," Lester said. "But I think it can't be a choice. Who in his right mind would choose a life of being shunned by the mainstream?" He shook his head to stress the point. "Nope, it's got to be something in the wiring."

"So my dad was born that way?"

"I'd say so. Doesn't mean you'll be that way. Genetics and biology are crazy, complex things—probably more than we'll ever know."

"You think it's immoral to be gay?"

Lester paused for a moment, and then he said, "You've got some bad thoughts brewing in that brain of yours."

"I just found out my dad's gay. What do you expect?"

"If it makes you feel any better, no, I don't think it's immoral. It's just a trait—somewhere between skin color and tastes for certain foods."

"I've heard people say it's immoral, like a sin, or a curse from God."

"Well, you're smart enough not to hang with that camp."

True, Alex thought, but it felt good to hear it from someone he respected instead of just sitting in silence, replaying his own negative thoughts. "So you think my dad might be okay?"

"Kid, I don't know about him personally. But if someone's willing to go out and face the world with that hanging over him and still be successful, he's got to have some fortitude."

"I never thought about it that way."

"Well, maybe that's the way you ought to think about it."

Alex nodded slowly. It was good advice. Then he looked at Lester. "When are you going to tell me why you never got married?"

"If you're thinking I'm gay, you're wrong. I like women fine. It's just that they don't care for me...at least not a certain part of me."

They passed the exit for Gainesville and the University of Florida. "What do you mean?"

Lester sighed. "I'm sure I'll be sorry for telling you this, because nothing good'll come of it."

Alex didn't reply.

"You want to know why I never got married."

It wasn't a question, but Alex said, "Yeah."

"All right," Lester said. "I got me a small pecker. That's it. That's the reason."

No comment from Alex.

"It's okay," Lester said. "You can laugh."

"I don't want to laugh."

"There's a stereotype about black men being well hung. Well, I'm here to tell you, it ain't always so."

Alex was silent. It was the most uncomfortable conversation they'd had so far. He would have preferred talking about death.

"I've had three embarrassing sexual encounters," Lester went on. "First one—Gwendolyn was her name—said, 'Is that all?' when she looked at it. Right out of the gate, that's what she said. Second woman, I don't remember her name, but I do remember the feeling. Like I was tossing a hot dog down a hallway. Not sure if that speaks worse of her or me. Last woman was a nurse. When we finished, she said I could've used a finger cot instead of a condom—you know what a finger cot is?"

"No," Alex said. "But I can guess."

"Never you mind," Lester said. He gave an awful wince. "Anyway, I figured three strikes you're out. That's what I figured."

"I've never had sex," Alex said.

"Don't be too eager."

WHEN THEY stopped for the night, Alex made a priority of starting his new exercise regime by swimming twenty laps in the over-chlorinated pool and hammering out twenty poolside push-ups. His arms gave out after fifteen, forcing him to do the last five girl-style. He did stomach crunches on his wet towel then a series of stretches he knew from gym class. At last, breathless and satisfied, he announced that he was done.

The old man sat in a patio chair reading a section of paper. "That's good," he said. "Keep it up and you'll be the next Charles Atlas."

"Who's that?"

"Way before your time, kid." He set the paper aside. "Let's get us a healthy dinner to go along with your new lifestyle."

Later that night, Alex stood in front of the bathroom mirror, posing and flexing his slender muscles. He pictured their mass after six months of grueling work-outs. Biceps, triceps, traps and abs—all ripped with layers of muscle. Everyday he'd inch himself toward the powerhouse body of his dreams. It would be the kind of body girls like Britney Garrand would talk about and admire. Just the thought of it made him smile. He wouldn't settle for being anything less than a hundred-percent man.

Then he noticed something from his salad, probably a piece of spinach, trapped between his teeth. It made him feel ugly all over again.

AFTER CHECK-OUT they headed west and north through Georgia back country. Lester drove, taking occasional sips of coffee. Alex ate a complimentary motel banana.

The trees lining the highway were animated by a steady headwind, but there were only a few clouds. Alex's eyes settled on a field of white dots on black limbs. Orphaned white stuff had blown off and gathered into clumps along the shoulders of the highway. A few clumps skittered across the road.

"Is that cotton?" he asked.

"It is," Lester said, slowing the car and pulling over. "Grab yourself a piece."

Alex got out and tracked a small wad that was whiter and puffier than the surrounding pieces. Back in the car, he examined it. There were a couple of hard seeds, but the rest was like a miniature pillow. Lester pointed to the piece and said, "There's a dark side to what you're holding."

"Okay," Alex said, bracing himself for the upcoming lecture.

"Aren't many cotton farms around here these days, but for generations that was our money crop." He cast an open hand across the windshield. "Hundreds of thousands of acres of cotton, hundreds of thousands of slaves to tend it. Entire Southern economy was based on cotton production. And for a long time the South was the world leader. King of the crop."

Alex rubbed the puffy wad between his thumb and forefinger.

"Meanwhile," Lester went on, raising a professorial finger, "the North was becoming an industrial power. Slaves weren't needed for the northern economy to thrive. Fact, slavery was becoming a worldwide embarrassment. That's how you had such a split in this country—cotton-farming, slave-dependent South, industrial North. They could've been on different planets."

"I thought the war was because people in the north had better values than the people down south."

"You thought wrong," Lester said. "One thing you ought to know—north, south, black or white—economics trumps values. Remember that next time you open a history book."

Alex said, "Will do." He was grateful not to be talking about death or undersized penises.

CHAPTER SIXTEEN

As they entered the town of Terrell, Alabama (population 925, according to a pockmarked sign) Lester was full of chatter about the old days compared to the way things were now. They drove up Main Street, but it wasn't called Main Street anymore. It was renamed Martin Luther King Jr. Drive in 1982, according to Lester. There was also a new traffic light in the center of town that always flashed yellow one way, red the other.

The street had exactly five operational businesses: a barber shop, miniature post office, Laundromat, a two-pump gas station with a convenience store and, Lester's favorite, Ernie's Catfish Shack. There were also three Christian churches in town, an elementary school and a middle school. "If a kid lives here long enough to go to high school," Lester said, "he gets bused over to Union Springs, the county seat."

As they rolled through downtown, Lester looked right and did a scowling double-take, as if he'd spotted a vandal. Alex saw what had grabbed the old man's attention. In the gaps between buildings, a series of boxcars rusted away on an abandoned track. Each car was engulfed in a green ocean of vines.

"Looks like they've been here awhile," Alex said.

"Nearly thirty years. If the railroad company had taken them out when they promised, it would've been an easy job. Now, forget it." He swatted his hand in disgust. "If this town was even half white, those cars would've been long gone, along with that goddamn kudzu."

This gave Alex a guilty sting, as if his whiteness somehow connected him to the bigwigs at the railroad company. He kept looking, counting nine cars in various states of decay. He contemplated the history of the cars—what they had carried, where they'd been before. A small cutaway in the vines made him think of hoboes with kerosene lamps. The idea was thrilling and exotic. If he joined these mythical squatters, how long would it take his mother to find him?

The Laundromat seemed to mark the end of downtown. They went another block and turned left onto Grove. Lester pointed to several of the houses, reporting who he thought still lived there. Then he said, "Someone ought to come around here with a paintbrush or two...and a weed-whacker."

And the old man was right. It looked as if the residents of Terrell were competing over who could neglect their home the most. First prize: dinner for two at Ernie's.

"Doesn't look like your neighborhood," Lester said. "But this is home."

"It's not that bad." Alex searched for something positive. "Lots of trees."

"Those are magnolias, prettiest trees you'll find." Lester turned left onto a gravel driveway. "This is it," he said. Then he shook his head. "I'll be damned." Parked straight ahead was a red Scion with New York plates. "We got company."

"Whose car is that?" Alex asked, but then he remembered from his bedroom window, and it made him feel ridiculously nervous.

"That would be Miss Rebecca," Lester said, turning off the engine. "Let's go see what the fuss is about."

Alex didn't budge. He stared at the car then looked up at the old clapboard house. Meanwhile, Lester had retrieved his stick from the backseat and was on his way to the rear of the house. He stopped and turned. "Come on, kid."

Finally, Alex stepped out. There were two rickety steps up to the back door and a railing that didn't look sturdy enough to hang laundry, let alone support a grown man. Lester probably knew this because he held onto his stick and took the steps slowly. "Coming in," he said.

The door swung inward, and there was Rebecca wearing a white sleeveless shirt and beige slacks that stood out against the baby blue cabinets of the kitchen. "Mr. Bray," she said, "and Alex. You don't know how relieved I am to see the two of you."

"Fine seeing you too, Dixie Cup." Lester tapped his stick on the side of the house then stepped into the kitchen. "I'm more popular than I thought."

Alex was still outside, but he could hear an old woman saying, "Well, look at you," all filled with mock surprise. It must've been Earlene. She was sitting at the kitchen table with a half-empty glass of iced tea in front of her.

Across the table was a pretty black girl who rose out of her seat. "I'll help you up, ma'am," the girl said to Earlene. "So you can give your brother a proper greeting."

"Hey, sis, you look good," Lester said. But all Alex could see was fat. He guessed the old woman weighed 400 pounds—fifty apiece for her breasts. She could have strung together a couple of mop buckets for a bra.

Earlene took the pretty girl's hand and began to rise. "Why, thank you, Les. I had to lose me some weight. Otherwise I'd break Selma's back."

"Take it you're Selma." Lester looked at the girl. "Glad to meet you." He stepped forward and shook Selma's hand. Then he looked back at Alex. "Don't be shy, kid. Got us some fine women here to visit with."

Alex finally stepped past the door and waved to Earlene and Selma.

Rebecca patted Alex's shoulder. "You and I've got some talking to do."

He half expected his mother to pop into the room.

"Well, let's not make the boy nervous," Earlene said, now standing on her own. She gave Lester a hug, nestling her face against his. "So good to see you."

"Good seeing you too, sis." He hugged her, but his arms weren't long enough to make it all the way around.

Earlene sat back down and looked at Selma. "Would you mind pouring us some sweet tea?"

"Not at all, ma'am." The girl was polite.

"And how about getting another chair?" There were five people and only four chairs at the table. "This kitchen's too small."

"That's okay, Miss Earlene," Selma said. "Y'all sit. I'll stand."

"How'd you get such a lovely friend?" Lester asked Earlene.

"Selma's my very favorite home health aide. I thank the Lord everyday I got her."

"Believe I would too." Lester took a seat across from Earlene while Alex sat next to Lester. Rebecca sat opposite Alex.

"Don't let him butter you up," Rebecca said to Selma. "These two look like fine gentlemen indeed. But the truth is, they're fugitives." Her face remained stern.

"Here we go," Lester said, elbowing Alex. "Nothing she says'll spoil the good times we've had."

"That's right." Alex felt less nervous thanks to Lester—partner in crime.

"Well," Rebecca said, "while the two of you've been out gallivanting around the country, having a fine time, I've been hearing bloody murder from two sources."

"Let me guess." Lester applied another elbow. "One of them's his mother."

"That's right." Rebecca was staring at Lester. "The other is Elder Spring. The entire board of directors has their fingers pointed at me. You and I are still under contract, Mr. Bray. I'm responsible for your wellbeing. When you run off like this, I'm the one who suffers." She flipped her hands in the air. "You're making a fool out of me."

"Sorry about that, Dixie Cup. I had no intention of doing you wrong."

"Sorry won't take care of our problem."

"I figured," Lester said. "No one drives over a thousand miles for an apology."

"She didn't drive straight through," Earlene said. "Isn't that right, Rebecca?"

"Well, that is true," Rebecca said. "I saw my folks in Marietta first."

"Now it's starting to make sense," Lester said, looking at his sister. "While I was in the hospital, recovering from my coma, you and

Rebecca developed a nice little friendship. And you tipped her off as to when we were coming."

"I had to, Les," Earlene said. "You got to be honorable by these people. Live up to what you agreed."

Lester took a long sip of tea and said, "Ah, that is good." Then he gave Alex another nudge and pointed to Earlene. "One year older and she thinks she's got lifelong rights to lecture me. You're lucky you're an only child."

"Oh, Les," Earlene said. "Lord knows there ain't enough lectures for you."

Lester seemed to glare for a moment then turned to Rebecca, "Let's see what else the lovely Dixie Cup has to say."

Rebecca talked as if she'd come well prepared. "First off," she said, "I'm happy to see the two of you are in good health. I was worried."

"Amen," said Earlene.

"Second thing is where we go from here. By running off, Mr. Bray, you put yourself in violation of our contract." She steadied her brown eyes upon him. "But I was able to talk the board into letting you back," she raised a finger, "under one condition."

Alex wondered why Lester would want to try living with another family after the current fiasco. But Lester merely looked at Rebecca and said, "I'm listening," like he was under her spell.

"You've got to be back in Albany before the close of business Friday. Today's Tuesday, in case you lost track."

Lester took another sip of tea while Rebecca crossed her arms. The silence was jarring, like an Iranian nuke standoff. Neither party was going to come away happy.

"I think we can manage," Lester finally said. "If we leave Thursday, that'll give us two nights and one full day in my hometown. Not much, but it'll do." Then he leaned forward and said, "Does this mean you got another family lined up?"

"I might, as long as you don't mess it up."

"If I didn't know better, I'd say you're angry with me." Now Lester crossed his arms to match hers. "You're too sweet to be angry…doesn't sit well with you."

"I'm not the only one who's angry," Rebecca said, now turning to Alex. "Your mother's about fit to be tied. That's the other reason I'm here."

"I'm glad it's you and not her," Alex said.

"That's what we social workers are all about, doing other people's dirty work."

"Nothing dirty about what we're doing," Lester said. "We're having a nice summer vacation, pure and simple. If that bitch of a mother he's got was a little less controlling and a little more understanding, we wouldn't be having these problems. Ain't that right, kid?"

"Exactly," Alex said.

"My Lord!" Earlene was staring at Lester. "You can't talk about the boy's mother that way."

"You haven't met her, sis."

"All right, enough," Rebecca said. "Regardless of what you think, she is his mother, and she wants him back." She looked at Alex. "But she can be reasonable. She was kind enough to let you drive up with Mr. Bray, as long as you're home by Friday evening."

"And what if we're not?" Alex asked. As strange as the trip was so far, he didn't want it to end.

"Then you'll both be in some serious trouble. Mr. Bray will have no place to stay, and he'll be looking at kidnapping charges. And you'll have to deal with your mother's consequences. I don't think they'll be pleasant."

"So," Lester said. "We're all agreed. We get back Friday. That gives us time for a nice little visit." He raised his glass of tea.

Alex raised his glass to Lester. It was a triumphant moment of sorts, but the thought of the old man ending up homeless threw Alex back to feeling guilty over the deal he'd made with his mother. Earlene and Rebecca raised and clinked their glasses.

"Sweetheart," Earlene said to Rebecca, "I do hope you'll be staying for supper. Selma's making smothered chicken, and I've already made pineapple upside down cake."

"Thank you so much, Earlene," Rebecca said. "But I have to be moving on. I'm afraid I've been neglecting the rest of my caseload because of these two." She pointed across the table.

Rebecca hugged everyone, including a tight embrace for Alex, which made him want to hop into her little red Scion and stare at her all the way up to New York.

LESTER AND EARLENE sat across from each other at the kitchen table reminiscing about things Alex had no interest in. He felt the sinking approach of boredom. Selma pulled a broom from the gap between wall and fridge and began sweeping. Alex's thoughts turned to dinner and how they'd manage to eat in this cramped kitchen while there seemed to be an ample-sized dining room next to it. But when he got up from the table and stepped into the adjacent room, he knew the reason. "There's a bed in here," he said to no one in particular.

Selma was standing behind him. She rested the broom against the door jamb. "That's where Miss Earlene sleeps. Stairs got to be too much."

In addition to the bed, there was a nightstand, a floor lamp and three piles of newspapers stacked about as high as Alex's waist. A little nudge and they'd landslide out onto the blemished floorboards. On the opposite side of the room stood an old dresser painted glossy brown with runs and brush marks. There were about a dozen medicine bottles clustered on one half of the dresser top and nearly a dozen framed photos on the other side. It felt too personal to look at them.

He turned back to Selma. "She doesn't use the second floor at all?"

"Twice a week, I help her up for a bath. There's just the half-bath down here." She pointed to a narrow door in the kitchen.

Alex wondered how anyone could survive on two baths per week. Then his mind went to where it always seemed to go when he was talking with pretty females.

Although he wasn't privy to scientific data on the topic, he came to believe that black girls, on average, had larger breasts than those of white girls. And the God of Breasts was particularly kind to Selma. Alex's eyes lingered at the grapefruit-size protrusions propping up her lime green shirt. Citrus Heaven. How he'd love to see those beauties in full glory. The mental snapshot brought him to full erection.

How could it happen so quickly? He had to think of something else. Then it struck him. "Selma," he said. "Isn't there a city named that?"

"Course there is," she said. "That's how I got my name—March on Selma, 1965, way before I was born, of course, but my grandma was there, and Dr. King was there. They called it Bloody Sunday, because the white troopers shot at us and beat us. But that's what led to us getting our rights." When she said these words, her chin became more prominent. She looked proud.

Alex no longer felt hot in the crotch. Instead he felt ashamed for thinking of her that way. This girl—woman, actually—was something special. "Have you been to Selma?" he asked.

"Quite a few times," she said. "There's a bridge where the march started and where things got ugly, but the people kept on walking. It's a good place to visit." She crossed her hands over her chest. "It stirs our souls."

Alex felt proud of himself for being able to focus on her words and not on the place where her hands had just gone. He was becoming more mature.

"Tell you what," she said, placing the broom back to its original slot, "let's get your bags into the house before supper. Rain's coming."

He followed her through the kitchen while Lester and Earlene debated who had the worst medical ailments. Lester seemed to be dominating the contest until Earlene pulled back her sleeve, revealing a hideous scar that ran from the bottom of her sagging arm to someplace Alex didn't care to know about.

"That's nothing," Lester said, "just cosmetics."

Outside, Alex opened the trunk and pulled out his duffel bag with one hand and Lester's old Samsonite with the other.

"I can help," Selma said.

"I'm fine, you just get the trunk."

She slammed the trunk. "You can't carry both those all the way upstairs."

"Sure I can." He began lumbering his way forward, step by awkward step.

She got in front and held open the kitchen door. "If I didn't know any better, I'd say you were showing off." She capped off her words with a smile.

It was true, he realized, and it made him flush. Thankfully, she marched ahead, passing through the makeshift bedroom and into the living room. She stopped at the foot of the stairs. "You ought to let me carry one of those bags. It's steeper than you think."

"I can manage," he said. Although the luggage had become unmercifully heavy, he wasn't about to wimp out. "I'm working on getting into better shape." It was totally the wrong thing to say.

She smirked then glided up the stairs, humming a playful melody.

There were three steps up to a landing. Turn left. Another seven or eight at an insanely steep pitch. He took the first three by storm then rested the bags on the landing. His breathing sounded almost like Lester's. He pivoted his body and bags for the final ascent. Lightning flashed about the room. Then the growl of thunder, just as Selma had predicted. He lunged forward, pulling and dragging the bags, each step making its own prehistoric crackle. A few seemed to pop under excess pressure, but they held strong. And Alex was feeling strong. He stood with the bags at the top of the staircase. Victorious.

"Took you long enough," she said. "I could've taken a nap up here."

"Funny," he said, but couldn't think of a decent comeback.

"There's three bedrooms, but only two still got beds in'em. I recommend you take this one here." She pointed to the room at the front of the house, directly above the living room.

"You're the boss," he said.

"Ooh, I like the sound of that."

A roar of thunder, and then the rain began pounding the house. Just like it had pounded Lester's Cadillac in Statesville. But instead of driving lessons, he got a cooking lesson, courtesy of Selma. And he got to sit across from her at dinner and sneak looks at her the whole time. If she had noticed, she didn't say anything. And no one got into trouble over his roving eyes. It was a sweet evening.

CHAPTER SEVENTEEN

The single item on Alex's morning agenda was to find a decent place to exercise. He made his way down to the kitchen where Earlene and Lester sat across from each other, reading sections of the *Montgomery Advertiser.*

"Good morning, Alex," Earlene said. "Such a glorious day after all that rain."

"It's bright out there," Alex said. He stopped in front of the fridge without opening the door.

"Don't be shy," Earlene said. "Get yourself whatever you'd like."

"Thanks, I'll just have juice."

Lester surveyed Alex up and down. "You look like you're ready for the decathlon, kid."

"I thought I'd go for a run."

"You'll get some looks if you run on the sidewalk."

"Where's a good place?"

"Here's what you do," Lester said, lowering his paper. "Go down to the middle school. It's three blocks that way." He pointed away from the center of town. "Last I remember they had a decent track. Run on that."

Earlene reached across the table and touched Lester's hand. "You don't think he'll want to join us?"

"Nah," Lester said, half to Earlene half to Alex. "All we're doing is driving around visiting some geriatrics and a cemetery. Kid's got a better plan. Let him be."

"Yeah, I'll pass," Alex said as he filled a glass with orange juice.

"Well, Selma should be arriving around nine," Earlene said. "You can keep her company till we get back."

"Sounds good," Alex said. And suddenly a day in Terrell, Alabama, didn't seem that bad.

Lester turned to the business of ridiculing his sister. He pointed to her bedroom and said, "What you doing with all those newspapers anyway?"

"I keep 'em for reminiscing."

"You ought to get yourself a computer. Less of a fire hazard."

"I don't smoke, and I don't light candles. I like things the way they are."

"World's changing fast." He sipped his coffee. "You're a dinosaur, sis."

"I do fine with my paper."

Lester shook his head. "Let me have a look at that sports section."

Dueling dinosaurs, Alex thought, as he stepped outside. Everything was wet and glistening under cloudless brilliance. The gravel driveway had turned into a patchwork of puddles and isthmuses. He walked a roundabout route to the front of the house and followed the sidewalk. Already he could feel that the day would be sweltering.

Three blocks, and there stood Terrell Middle School. It was a white saltbox, two stories high, with chipped paint and shutters that looked like they'd blast apart in a stiff breeze. A square cupola was centered atop the building—its clock stopped at three-thirty. If the school was even half white, Alex figured, the clock probably would've read quarter-after-eight. He was starting to think like Lester.

A vacant playground, still dripping wet, stretched along the shade of the school, and the track was behind the schoolhouse and playground. There was a black boy, probably eleven or twelve, running suicide sprints in the grassy center. The boy wore neon orange cleats that looked fresh out of the box. Alex gave a half-wave and began running clockwise.

He settled into a pace that seemed manageable for a long distance run—challenging enough to work his cardiovascular system, but not so fast that he'd have to stop and pant and embarrass himself in front of the boy. As he rounded the second bend, he noticed that the boy had four Gatorade bottles spaced evenly along the length of the field. The first bottle served as home-base. The boy ran from home to the second bottle, reached down, touched it, then he ran back to home. He ran to the third bottle, touched it, and so on. The kid had been running before Alex arrived, so there was no telling how many cycles he had completed. But a narrow streak of ripped grass from the first to fourth bottle suggested he'd been at it awhile.

By lap three, Alex was sweating and breathing vigorously. He cut his speed slightly. Meanwhile, the boy kept sprinting—far faster, Alex knew, than he'd ever be able to run. It didn't help that his left heel began aching, and he was thirsty to the point of lightheadedness. After completing lap twelve, he decided to call it quits. He slowed to a jog and stopped at a bench where he did a series of push-ups, sit-ups and stretches. While lying with his back twisted away from the field, he heard grassy footsteps approaching. "What you doing wearing shoes like that for running? Them are basketball shoes."

Alex turned to face the speedster boy. "They're all I brought with me."

"Want some Gatorade?" The boy extended a bottle toward him. It was half-filled with green fluid.

Alex immediately thought of germs and germ-borne illnesses. Then he figured the kid wanted money. "I can't pay."

"No charge," the boy said.

Alex uncapped the bottle, suppressed all thoughts of disease and drank the contents in one swig. It was warm but satisfying. He looked up at the boy and said, "You've got some serious speed."

"I know," the boy said. "My uncle says I'm gonna be the next Bo Jackson. I'll go pro after my junior year at Auburn, and I'll buy everyone I like a mansion."

"Who's Bo Jackson?"

The boy looked at Alex all screw-faced. "Where you from?"

"Upstate New York," Alex said, "Albany."

"Man, you New Yorkers don't know nothin'." He took the empty bottle from Alex's hand and walked away.

Alex rose to his feet and noticed that his heel was still bothering him. The boy was right. The shoes were all wrong for running. He'd have to limp his way back to Earlene's house.

Up ahead, he could see four black kids hanging out on the sidewalk. As he got closer, he saw that one of them was a girl. She was dribbling a basketball, talking louder than the others, like she was the leader. The others were boys, all about Alex's age, maybe older. Half a block away, he realized the group wasn't about to step aside for him.

He'd have to make a semi-circle onto someone's lawn or out onto the street. His thoughts shifted to getting life from the shitty end of the stick. He pictured himself poor and black and stuck in a town with no opportunity. As he began circumnavigating the group, one of them said, "Hey." But Alex was lost in his own mental picture.

"I said hey, boy!" same voice only louder.

Alex heard it this time, but he was past the group. He looked back and said, "Hey."

The girl laughed and said, "You need to learn how to *re-lax*."

The words struck him immediately. Dr. Kruger could have said the same thing ten times, and it wouldn't have mattered. But it was different coming from her. She was totally right.

SELMA'S MALIBU was parked on the street in front of Earlene's house. Alex had watched her leave the previous evening from his bedroom window, watched her open the driver's side door. That's when she hesitated, looked up and smiled. He tried to make it look as if he was squinting at magnolia branches, like he was some budding arborist. A lame attempt, and the embarrassment was still fresh.

It would be another source of embarrassment if she got close to him, sweating and stinking the way he did. He hoped to make a dash for the upstairs shower without interference, but the front door was locked. So he gimped past the shrinking puddles in the driveway and peered through the kitchen door window. There was Selma washing dishes at the sink. No chance of avoiding her. He opened the door and entered.

She turned off the faucet and looked at him. "Saw you limping," she said. "You hurt yourself?" She was wearing a pink t-shirt, sleeveless and form-fitting.

"Not really," he said. "I just ran with the wrong kind of shoe."

She looked down at his high-tops and smirked. "And here I thought you were smarter than that."

"Apparently not." He passed by her on the opposite side of the table.

"You're still leaving tomorrow?"

"That's right," Alex said. "Why?"

"Just wondering."

"I've gotta take a shower." He turned away from her.

"I'll wait to wash the rest of the dishes then."

Puzzled, he stopped in the middle of Earlene's bedroom and looked back into the kitchen. "Why would you do that?"

"Because the water pressure'll be way off for your shower."

"Oh," he said, "thanks." He shook his head wondering what other quirks the old house had.

The pipes groaned and clattered as he tested the water and stepped into the scarred enamel tub. He couldn't take his mind off her. As soon as the warm water struck his penis, it was bone-hard. He could masturbate, just to get rid of the pressure. But then he pictured her downstairs waiting to re-start the dishes, judging him harshly for taking such a long shower. It was no good.

Freshly cleaned, he dried himself off and pushed his saluting penis under the confines of his towel. He angled his body away from the staircase and opened the bedroom door. Then he shut it behind him. Something told him to lock the door. So he locked it.

"I was going to tell you to do that." It was Selma's voice.

He turned toward the bed. She was lying under the white sheet. Her whole body covered except for her head. "Can you keep a secret?" she asked.

His chest felt as if it were caving in on him, and his face was flushed, probably looked ridiculous.

"Can you keep a secret?" she repeated.

"Yeah," he said. "I can...definitely." He was afraid that if he spoke at any length, his words would come out all pureed and stupid.

"I can't lose this job. You have to swear."

"Yeah," he said. "I swear, honestly." And he meant it.

"Okay," she said. "Drop the towel and slip yourself in." She flipped down the nearest corner of sheet and slid away to make room. "I brought condoms." She continued speaking, but he barely registered. He released the towel. His penis was staring straight at her. All he could think was that very soon he'd be seeing those breasts with his own eyes and touching them with his very own hands.

"Come on," she said. "We may not have much time."

He slid into bed, practically dove into it. His hand reached for her. He felt the side of her. She was naked. "No fair," he said. "You already saw me. I can't see you."

She glared at him. "Men are so visual. Doesn't matter if you're black or white." She raised her left leg clear of the sheet. "I guess you deserve a peek." Then she pointed her slender toes toward the ceiling and cranked her foot a couple of times. "Happy?"

"Very funny," he said, tugging at the sheet, but Selma held her grip.

"Okay, okay," she said. "Here you go, have yourself a look." Her hands fiddled with the condom box. His shining moment had arrived. He tossed the sheet clear of the bed and stared along the profile of her perfect body. Her nipples shone under the light of the window. They were so black they were purple. He could tell that his penis was already leaking fluid. He cupped his hand over one breast and stared at the other.

She turned toward him. "Your first time, right?"

Somehow the power of conversation had left him. A moment passed. Then he managed to say, "How'd you know?"

"I could tell, the way you carry yourself." She handed him a condom. "Put this on. Make sure you got it on good."

He turned away from her and unraveled the slimy thing onto his erection. "Okay, ready," he said.

"Good, you get on top." She moved to the center of the mattress and spread her legs. Her hips gyrated side to side. She was rubbing herself with one hand and a nipple with the other.

He crawled halfway over, stopped and ushered himself forward. He prodded himself into her. She was hot inside. The feeling was amazing. More amazing than he could have imagined. He tried to look at her eyes, but they were closed.

He lowered his head next to hers and thrust himself forward. Once. Twice. A third time. Some powerful force shifted inside him. His whole body turned ecstatic. He let out a long "Aaahh," and then, "oh, oh, oh."

He pulled himself out and collapsed next to her. He was soaking with sweat.

Selma returned to rubbing herself while gyrating her hips. Her eyes were still closed. She gave a gentle moan. It dawned on him that he hadn't completely satisfied her with his penis. He looked down at the thing now curled onto his left thigh like a beige Cheez Doodle. It looked pathetic. He pulled off the rubber.

She was still doing her thing with her fingers and her hips. "So," he cleared his throat, "what did you think?"

Her eyes were still closed. "It was fine."

"You sure? I wasn't too quick? 'Cause I think I was too quick." The words stampeded out of him.

"Relax," she said. "You did fine. You'll last longer once you get the hang of it."

"Did you like it?"

"Course I did. It was fun." Her hips were still going at it.

"No, I mean...." He was too embarrassed to say what he really meant.

She turned and finally opened her eyes. "What you wanna say?"

There didn't seem to be anything dangerous about her. He might as well ask. "Okay," he said, "I was just wondering if you thought my... my *thing* was big enough."

Her face broke into a smile. "So that's what you're so concerned about."

"Not really," he said. He looked up at the ceiling. "Well, maybe a little."

She reached down and gave his limp penis a little squeeze. "I think it's fine," she said, "just fine." Her hand began pulling at it.

And then, like a bicycle tire, it slowly inflated. Ready for another ride.

Selma gave him a new condom, and he was like an old pro getting the thing on. This time, she got on top. He watched her boobs jiggle and dance, up and down, round and round. She was moaning and breathing hard. He wanted it to last for her. So he looked up at the dusty light fixture, trying to think of something totally non-arousing. But no more than a minute passed before he was done and trembling.

She reached for the base of his penis, held onto the condom and pulled herself away. "Skootch over," she said.

He gave her the majority of the bed so that she could resume with her rubbing and her gyrations. Here was an image he hoped would last a lifetime.

"Want to do something a little different?" she asked.

"Yeah, definitely," he said without thinking.

"Put your head down here." She pointed her index finger, and she winked.

He was completely under her command. She could have had him woof-woofing for dog biscuits. He hopped out of bed, went around and planted his face into her crotch.

"Right here," she said, pressing a certain spot.

He knew enough to lick vigorously. It seemed odd to be licking around the same vicinity where his penis had just gone. But it wasn't enough to make him stop. His new mission in life was to give her the same kind of pleasure he'd just received.

In a little while, Selma was moaning as loudly as a yell. There weren't any real words, just ooh's and aah's then one long H-a-a-a-a-a-ah that lasted nearly half a minute. He kept his mouth pressed against her. Each hand held an ass cheek. His eyes stared up at the top half of her body, now flapping and flailing around as if in need of an exorcist. She pushed his head away. Her body slowed down. She returned to her original half of the bed. It was an invitation to lie next to her.

"That was amazing," she said as she turned and held his face between her hands. Then she kissed him on the lips. It was their first kiss.

"Good," he said. "I'm glad."

"Keep that up and I'll have to start calling you Alexander the Great."

He felt himself getting flush all over again. He couldn't fathom such a title, especially coming from her. She was the great one.

They lay there holding each other for a while. Then there was the unmistakable sound of tires on gravel followed by Cadillac doors opening and slamming shut.

"You know why I chose this room for you?" She started dressing herself.

"Not really," he said, wrestling things out of his duffel bag.

"Cause the floor doesn't squeak as badly as the other."

"Wow," he said. "So you knew even then?"

She shot him a scolding look. "And you thought you were the superior sex."

All he could think to say was, "Woof-woof."

CHAPTER EIGHTEEN

What's a person supposed to do after the most thrilling event of his life? If it were up to Alex, the town would hold a parade with floats and marching bands in honor of Selma. A team of reporters with cameras would demand a play-by-play summary after which Alex would place a crown atop Selma's head. *Miss Sexuality.* Then, as finale, he'd cartwheel from boxcar to boxcar. Anything less wouldn't do it justice.

But after dressing and making it safely downstairs, he found himself sitting in a rocking chair between two ancient sleepers. To his right was Earlene in a recliner, snoring like a sow held underwater. Lester was comparatively quiet, lying on the couch with his head cocked toward the off television. Selma was busy in the kitchen making up for the time she'd spent with Alex.

His sketchpad lay before him. He wanted to draw a picture of Selma, of course, all naked and radiant. But that could get her fired, and maybe land him a permanent display in the Alabama Hall of Shame. So he picked something totally asexual. He started with a couple of rectangles and a series of circles. A leaf here and there. It was starting to take shape. He kept going.

Lester turned and gave a half-groan, half-yawn. He sat up and looked over at Alex. "What you drawing?"

"It's not done yet." He was shading a section of foreground.

"Let me see it anyway."

Alex displayed a partial rendering of boxcars being swallowed by giant killer weeds.

"Surreal," Lester said. "Very nice tribute to the town."

Earlene was starting to wake up. She let out a high pitch "Whew." Then she yawned, just like her brother, while fidgeting with the side of her chair. She must have noticed Alex's drawing, because she said, "My, what a talented boy."

"Thanks," Alex said. "It's not done yet."

Lester's eyes lingered at Alex's face for an uncomfortably long moment. "What you keep smiling about?"

"Nothing," Alex said. He tried to erase the smile, but it was probably still there. "I had a nice run. It's not bad here."

"Well, too bad for you, we're leaving tomorrow."

The reminder took away the smile. "I was wondering," he said to Lester, "who's Bo Jackson?"

"You kidding me," Lester said. "You don't know who Bo Jackson is?"

"Nope."

"Well, shit." Lester slapped his leg. "Bo Jackson is only the greatest running back ever to play college football."

Earlene let out a groggy, "Amen."

"And he was one hell of a great baseball player too."

"Amen," Earlene repeated.

"Oh," Alex said, "I was just wondering."

Lester stared at him. "What makes you wonder about a thing like that?"

"It was this boy I saw at the track. He was fast, I mean really fast. His uncle told him he'd be the next Bo Jackson."

"And you told that boy you didn't know who Bo Jackson was." Lester shook his head as if a sacred code had been violated.

"That's right."

"You must've felt like a moron."

"I did," Alex said, "but I got over it."

"You look like you got over it pretty good," Lester said. "You look happy. Doesn't he, Earlene?"

"I guess he does," she said. "The South suits him."

"You been drinking?" Lester asked.

"No, I swear. I just had a good run. I'm starting to like running."

"Hell, if that's all it took, I'd have started running years ago."

Selma came into the room from the kitchen. "Y'all want some sweet tea?"

"Yes, darling," Earlene said. "That'd be so nice."

Selma nodded and returned to the kitchen.

"Now there's something that could make a man happy," Lester said.

"Hush your mouth!" Earlene said, giving him a brutal look. "We got an impressionable here. You ought to watch what you say."

"Easy, old girl," Lester said. "I say we go out with a bang tonight. Let's all go to Ernie's and get us some catfish." He gave his stomach a circular rub. "You up for that, kid?"

"I guess so."

"Not for me," Earlene said. "All that grease, and it's one step closer to the grave." She shooed her hand in the direction of Lester and Alex. "You boys go on, enjoy yourselves."

"I believe that's what we'll do," Lester said. Then he lowered his voice. "Think I should invite Selma to come along?"

"She'll be fine with me," Earlene said. "Girl's only eighteen, pure and good. I don't want you corrupting her."

Alex could feel himself smiling again, so he closed his sketchpad and started for the stairs.

"Just trying to be polite," Lester said.

When Alex returned, there was only Earlene in the recliner. Lester was in the kitchen talking quietly with Selma. Impossible. He tried to sharpen his hearing, but all he could make out was the old man saying, "The kid's birthday," then nothing but a whisper.

"THE SIGN'S NEW," Lester said from the passenger seat. He was pointing to the plastic neon fish with Ernie's Catfish Shack printed across the belly. "Hope that's the only new thing. I don't want some diversified, heart-smart menu. I want the same-old, same-old." He opened his door. "I want grease."

Alex jogged around to help Lester. "Here, take my hand," he said.

"I can get myself out."

"Just trying to be helpful."

"Well, you can help by getting my stick."

No sooner did Lester speak the words than Alex had the stick poised for operation. "Thanks," Lester said. "Now get the door." He nodded at the patrons in window-side booths who appeared to be staring at the two of them. "Folks must think you're my hired help. Wouldn't that be something?"

Alex held open the door. "Okay by me."

"You're not even a little scared about dining at an all-black restaurant?"

"No problem."

Lester stepped inside. A stumpy woman with a yellow bonnet covering her afro pulled two menus out of a bin and said, "Booth or counter?"

"Booth," Lester said.

She turned and marched toward the back of the restaurant. The place reeked of grease and cornmeal and cigarettes, and it was loud and nearly capacity filled. But none of this bothered Alex. He felt like a different person altogether. And a better one. As if Selma had granted him a kind of superhuman power—the power of cool confidence. Lester made an ordeal out of stopping along the way at a framed photo of Bo Jackson who was posing with his Heisman Trophy. "There's your man," he said.

At the booth, Lester sat down with his back to the restrooms. "Since I'm buying, I'll take the better view."

"Fine with me," Alex said.

A waitress arrived to take their drink order. She was much more attractive than the hostess, but when she opened her mouth there were big buckteeth like jagged piano keys sticking out of her top gums. It was a shame to have that as your defining feature. Alex silently pledged not to stare at her mouth but to appreciate her finer assets.

"Think we'll both have sweet tea," Lester said as he opened his menu. "That okay with you, kid?"

"Yeah, that's fine."

"Be right back," the waitress said.

Lester looked at his menu while talking to Alex. "You basically got two choices—beer battered catfish or cornmeal catfish fillets. Both are fried, and both are delicious. Can't go wrong. I say you pick one, I pick the other, and we share."

"Sounds fine," Alex said.

"Everything's good here, but you may want to steer clear of the fried okra. If you're anything like me, it'll turn your intestines to music."

Alex smiled. "I'll avoid it."

The waitress set down two tea-filled mason jars and pulled out a pad to record their order.

"I'll have the beer-battered," Lester said. "He'll have the cornmeal fillets. I'll have black eyed peas and a big old square of that corn bread. Bring extra butter."

She took his menu and turned to Alex. "I'll have baked beans and a tossed salad." He handed her the menu.

Lester sucked down a long sip of tea. Then he said, "Nectar of the gods."

More like *diabetes in a jar*, Alex was about to say, but he didn't want to ruin the good mood. He shifted the conversation. "I was thinking about catfish," he said. "I've never had it before, because I've always thought of them as bottom feeders."

"Well, that's basically what they are," Lester said.

"Right, but I was thinking about when you told me not to pick my nose."

"Why in the hell would you bring that up?"

"It's kind of the same thing. Catfish and boogers are both like pool skimmers."

Lester shook his head in obvious disgust. Then he stared at Alex. "There's definitely something different about you." He kept staring.

Alex didn't respond. The waitress arrived with two platters of food. She set them down and said, "Anything else I can do for you?"

"Yeah," Lester said, pointing at Alex. "Tell me what's gotten into this kid. He's been acting strange today."

As if to take the request seriously, she gave Alex a steady look. Then she said, "I'd say he's been foolin' around." She smiled her fanged smile and walked away.

"Huh," Lester said.

"That's ridiculous." Alex's face was hot enough to sauté onions.

"What did you do this afternoon while we were gone?"

"Nothing," Alex said, "I ran, like I told you. Then I just sat around."

"I think maybe you were messing with that home health aide."

"Come on," Alex said, "that's crazy."

"You dog." Lester forked a piece of catfish and blew on it. "So how was she?"

"She wasn't anything. We didn't do anything."

"Try again." Lester blew once more. "How was she?"

Alex shook his head but then finally whispered, "No one can know. I swore I wouldn't tell. She could get fired."

"Nobody's gonna know. It's just you and me having a chat." The old man popped the bite into his mouth. He chewed while closing his eyes. "Ah, that is good," he said. "Just like I remember—tangy, a little spicy, with a back-end of sweetness."

Alex was mortified at being discovered. "I don't think I should say anymore."

"Kid, you keep quiet and you'll explode from all the pressure. You got to tell at least one person. Might as well be me."

Alex peered sideways then to the booth behind. He kept his voice just above a whisper. "It was the most amazing thing ever."

Lester nodded and chewed another piece of beer-battered catfish. "I'm glad it was, kid. Glad it was."

Alex started on his fish, which was truly delicious. He regretted the booger analogy. And then he thought about Lester's private conversation with Selma. "So what were the two of you talking about?"

Lester didn't even bother looking up from his plate. "Now that's none of your goddamn business."

CHAPTER NINETEEN

Alex's dreams were filled with Selma. One featured him racing through mountains on a motorcycle. She sat behind, left hand pressed against his chest while her other hand fiddled with his zipper. The excitement was too much. Up ahead—a paralyzed elk in the center of the road. The motorcycle smacked head-on, causing the animal to burst into milky fluid.

He bolted upright, sprang out of bed and over to the window, hoping to see the Malibu. But when he looked down through thick magnolia, all he could see was sun-speckled asphalt and potholes. So he lay back down and wondered what time Lester had planned for them to leave. If it was before nine, he'd miss her. Probably forever. He could stall, feign sickness or simply barricade himself in the room until she arrived.

The other problem was the aftermath of Ernie's Catfish Shack. The food was awesome, but he had eaten too much and was now bloated and farting away like a Taliban firing squad. How could he possibly get intimate with that going on?

It was no use. He went to the bathroom, showered and dressed for the day. Downstairs, he looked at the street from the living room window. Still no Selma.

"Good morning Alex." It was Earlene from the other end of the house. As usual, Lester sat across from her, reading a section of paper. God knows what these two would've done if the paper boy failed to show.

"Good morning," Alex said and poured himself a glass of orange juice.

"Another glorious day," Earlene said.

Alex rubbed his stomach. "I should go for another run, especially after all I ate."

"Kid was unstoppable," Lester said. "I warned him, told him his belly wasn't up to all that grease. But he kept going."

"I should've listened."

"Sometimes it's better to learn the hard way," Lester said.

"Praise be," Earlene said. "We know a few things about learning things the hard way. Don't we, Les?"

"That we do," Lester said, looking at his wristwatch. "We leave in twenty minutes...nine o'clock. My bag's already packed. Bring it down when you're ready."

The finality of leaving pressed hard against Alex's chest. But then he heard the sound he'd been waiting for. It was the distant sputter of the Malibu, the slam of her door and her footsteps on gravel. His heart leaped. He expected her radiant figure at the back door, but she lingered outside. He could hear her opening one of the Cadillac doors. Then she shut it.

"Must be Selma," Earlene said.

Alex swiped his upper front teeth with his tongue, licked his lips and roughed the hair at his forehead. There she stood at the landing with two bags of groceries. He bolted out of his chair, but she was inside before he had a chance to get to the door.

"You get an A for effort," she said.

"I can help you put things away."

"You'll do no such thing," Lester said. "Get those suitcases downstairs, and then you can say your goodbyes."

"I like that the boy wants to help," Earlene said, turning to Alex. "That's good Christian kindness on your part."

"Thanks," Alex said. "I'll be right back."

He took the stairs two at a time and practically flew to the back bedroom for Lester's suitcase. All he had to do was brush his teeth, pack toiletries into his duffel bag and he was downstairs with both bags, breathless.

Lester was leaning against the oven, stick in hand. He looked at Alex and said, "Took you three minutes. If I didn't know better, I'd think you wanted out of here."

"Funny," Alex said.

The old man winked. "Now you go on, give these two lovely ladies a proper hug, and we'll be on our way."

Earlene pushed herself halfway out of her chair. Selma helped her the rest of the way up. "Let's go outside, Miss Earlene. We'll see them off in the sunshine."

"I'm afraid they'll see me cry," Earlene said.

"That's all right." Selma's hands were slings under the old woman's elbows. "You cry all you need to."

Alex stayed in the kitchen while the others made their way to the driveway. He surveyed the paneled room one last time. It was sad to think this room was closer to his heart than the kitchen his mother kept.

Outside, he hoisted the luggage into the trunk. Earlene was already weeping in Selma's arms. Lester went over and placed a hand on the side of Earlene's face. "I don't imagine I'll see you again, sis. This is probably it."

Earlene's sobbing intensified. "Why you always have to be so truthful?"

Selma reached for Lester and pulled him toward Earlene. Brother and sister hugged while Selma stroked their backs. Meanwhile Alex leaned against the Cadillac and said nothing. Distance kept him from emotional display, but he could feel it coming.

Lester turned to Selma. "You do a fine job," he said. "You make my sister happy. And I thank you."

Tears were now streaming down Selma's face. "Thank you, Mr. Bray," she said. "Hope you got a lot of years left. And you'll come back this way."

It was Alex's turn to step into the arms of Earlene. She was soft and warm, like a big wet pillow, and her tears were still flowing. She gave him a gentle embrace. But then she followed with a squeeze that startled out a catfish fart before he could stop it.

"God bless you, child," she said. "You'll make a good man."

He wondered what kind of words she'd have if she knew what he and Selma had done. "Thanks for everything," he said. "I really enjoyed it."

Then he hugged Selma while whispering *thank you* into her ear.

She whispered back, "You're welcome." Then she added, "I got you a little something. It's behind the front seat. You open it when you're ready...not now."

The first feeling to strike him was guilt. "Thanks," he said, "but I didn't get you anything."

"You weren't supposed to." She broke away from the hug. "Now you be good. Make your momma proud."

In a minute's time, he had gone from grief to arousal to guilt then back to grief. He began to cry. All he could think to say was, "I'll make myself proud." Then he slipped into the passenger seat and looked once more at Selma and Earlene. Both were still crying. Lester's were the only dry eyes.

NORTH OF Union Springs, they detoured through the city of Tuskegee and the university, passing by the birthplace of Rosa Parks and the memorial home of Booker T. Washington. Lester drove slowly while talking about how the campus had looked fifty-five years earlier. "Nothing but a few buildings and a patchwork of farms," he said. "But I'll say this—it was a fine education."

Alex nodded, impressed by how clean and orderly the campus was. "I'm hoping to go to college."

"Damn straight you will. Can't do much of anything these days without it."

"I don't know where I'll go or what I'll study. I just know I need to go."

"If you're undecided, you ought to pick a big school, like Michigan or Penn State or even Syracuse. That way, you got lots of choices."

"I'll start researching it when I get home." Just saying the word *home* seemed to throw him into state of depression. Two more years with his mother loomed like a prison sentence. College would be a godsend.

They turned north and followed the signs to I-85. "Sightseeing's over," Lester said, "it's all interstate from here."

"Think I should open the gift?" Alex asked.

"If you want, but I recommend you wait. That way you can sit awhile longer with the mystery. It's nice to keep some mystery alive."

Alex uncapped a bottle of water. "You're right, I'll wait." He tore into a bag of cashews.

"I'd say you're maturing," Lester said.

"I don't want to be a scrawny punk all my life."

Lester shook his head. "You won't."

"How was your trip to the cemetery?" Alex's mouth was full of nuts.

"It was special. I had what you'd call an epiphany."

"What's that?"

"It's like a flash of understanding," Lester said. "I could envision the deaths of all my family members. Not just the ceremonies, but the actual deaths." They were back in familiar territory, driving and talking about Lester's favorite subject. He went on: "I got a better understanding, like I could see how each of them died, how they finally let go."

"Sounds pretty depressing," Alex said.

"Not as you might think. Thing is, they all needed somebody. And when they thought nobody was there anymore—when they truly felt alone—that's when they died. All my family members died alone."

"How could that not be depressing?"

"Because it's just the way it was. When you think there's no one left for you anymore, you pass on. That's usually how it goes. Unless you get hit by a Mack truck or a bad disease."

"I still say it's depressing."

"Well, you ought to get a broader perspective on death."

"What's more depressing than death?"

"I'll tell you," Lester said, waving a finger at Alex's face. "Living a shallow life. That's what."

ALEX REMAINED quiet for the stretch of highway leading into Georgia. The sign marking their transition from state to state only worsened his lovesickness over Selma. He wished he'd been driving so he could put his mind on something else. There were merger signs up ahead and warnings that the right lane was closed. Lester slowed the Caddy and drifted left.

But apparently he hadn't slowed down quickly enough. "Ah shit," he said. "We got a trooper on our ass."

Alex looked back. It approached from a hidden glade in the median strip, blue lights flashing. "That sucks," Alex said. "What are you gonna do?"

"I'm going to pull over, you knucklehead. What else would I do?" Lester drove to the end of the construction zone then pulled over. He looked at Alex and said, "Sorry, kid, you're not a knucklehead. I'm just angry."

"That's okay." Alex looked back and saw a big white trooper, full beard and mustache, rising out of his car and putting on his hat.

Lester lowered his window.

The trooper stood just shy of the door. "I'll have a look at your license and registration."

"What's the charge, sir?"

"Posted speed in the work zone is forty-five. Got you clocked at sixty-one."

Lester shrugged but didn't say anything. He pulled the license from his wallet then leaned toward the glove box, fingered through the contents and pulled out the registration slip.

"Stay in the car," the trooper said. "Be right back."

While they waited, Lester lowered all the windows. Then he

reached into the glove box and pulled out a sheet of paper. It was the notarized statement granting Alex ownership of the car. All it did was make Alex sad. Lester tucked it back and said, "Sometimes these things are worth arguing about. Other times, it just makes it worse. I'll have to wait and see when he comes back."

"I got a bad feeling," Alex said.

"Worst they can do is slap me with a steep fine. I'm old, but I'm not poor."

"So it's just a speeding ticket?"

"Call it what you like," Lester said. "Speeding or a DWB: driving while black."

It was the kind of remark Alex normally laughed at, but not this time. Twenty minutes of silence passed like the drifting of continents. Finally, there was movement. The big trooper's door slammed. Alex looked back. The man put on his hat. There was nothing in his hands, no citation.

He came to Lester's window. "Step out of the vehicle, sir—hands where I can see'em."

"What's this all about?"

"Out of the vehicle, now!" The trooper peered in at Alex. "You stay put."

Lester opened the door and pulled himself out.

"Hands on the side of the vehicle. I need to search you."

"What the hell's this about?"

"You have the right to remain silent—"

"I know my rights," Lester said. "Now tell me what's going on."

"You're under arrest for assaulting a police officer."

"Impossible," Lester said. But then he peered through the opened window at Alex. "Well, if that don't suck."

Alex's mind flashed back to the truck stop in Brunswick. The big racist boyfriend could have been a cop. And his final words: *I'm not through with you.* Alex's hands were trembling, his chest all knotted up. He couldn't bring himself to watch Lester getting patted down like a common criminal.

To the trooper Lester said, "Wait one minute."

Alex turned and saw the cop holding Lester's wallet.

"Sir," Lester said, "I need to give my friend some money or he'll never make it back home. Please allow me a minute with him."

"How old is he?"

"Seventeen, just turned. See that present right there?" Lester pointed to the package behind Alex's seat. "That's from his girlfriend."

"Is he legal to drive?"

"Course he is," Lester said. "Go on check if you like."

The trooper stooped to Alex's eye level. "What's your name, son?"

Alex cleared his throat. "Alex Riley." No chirp, thank God.

"Step out of the car."

Alex managed to get out and face the trooper. The man was almost a foot taller and probably 150 pounds heavier. For sport he could have tossed Alex's body into the air then shot it apart like a clay pigeon.

Lester pointed to the wallet in the mighty trooper's hand and said, "I need that back, please."

The trooper handed it over. "You're on borrowed time."

Lester pulled out some bills. "This is more than enough for gas and food and a motel," he said to Alex. There were four hundreds and a twenty. "Get yourself back to Albany. You'll be fine."

Alex's eyes started watering. He held the money all wrong, like the way you'd hold the string of a teabag. "I'm not leaving without you."

"Listen," Lester said, voice unnaturally loud. "You put that money in a safe place and get back in the car. You're not a part of this. There's no debate."

"He's given you good advice," the trooper said, pointing to the driver's door.

Tears streamed down Alex's face. He turned away from the two men and scooted into the car. He went from the driver's seat over to the passenger. He sat there for a moment. Then he drifted back over to the driver's seat.

A white K-9 van pulled in past the Cadillac and stopped. A female cop went around to the back of the van. "You're going to have a dog sniff me over?" Lester said. "That's ridiculous! Only drugs I have are the ones to keep me from dropping dead."

"The dog's headed for a homeland security facility in Brunswick," the trooper said. "Same town you're headed. That's your ride. Having her sniff out the vehicle might just keep me from having to tear it apart. That includes your friend's birthday gift."

A German shepherd jumped out. The female cop held the dog by the collar and said, "Here Ginger." Then a young male cop came out from the passenger side.

The big trooper pulled handcuffs from his belt and turned to Lester. "You'll have to wear these."

"Long drive to be wearing cuffs," Lester said.

The newest cop came over and said, "We're going to make it easy on you, Mr. Bray." He had a Hispanic accent. "We're only going to cuff one of your wrists to Ginger's cage."

"How's that going to be any easier?"

"It's better than having them behind your back for six hours. Trust me."

CHAPTER TWENTY

Alex's nerves had descended a couple of registers, from his chest down to his stomach and intestines. He sat with the Cadillac keys on his lap while Lester, now handcuffed and flanked by two cops, staggered his way to the van. There was a brief moment when the old man turned and nodded at Alex, as if to imply that everything was okay.

But Alex knew better. This was nearly as bad as things could get.

The female cop opened the door behind him and directed the dog to sniff out the entire area, including his present from Selma. "You'll have to step out of the vehicle," she said, her voice husky and false.

Alex peeked behind the driver's seat to verify that his gift was still there. That was the only good thing about the day. Then he stood in front of the car and watched through the windshield as the dog scurried across the seats.

The cop opened the trunk, and the dog jumped right in. Alex could hear the familiar snapping of the old Samsonite latches. This whole thing was terrible, and it was bound to get worse. The situation was clear: In a matter of seconds, one of the cops would demand to see his license. With only a learner's permit, he'd be nabbed as an illegal driver. The car would have to be impounded, and he'd be taken to some juvenile home until his mother arrived to claim him.

His wallet felt hot in his back pocket, like a grilled cheese sandwich straight off the burner. He didn't dare touch it. Except for his wobbling knees, he remained motionless, waiting for the inevitable.

"Is this yours?" the Hispanic cop asked, pointing to the green duffel bag.

"Yeah," Alex said.

The man tossed it back into the trunk. Meanwhile the big trooper carried Lester's suitcase to the van as if it was nothing but a box of Kleenex. Alex looked through the van's set of back windows, but all he could see was Lester's hand sticking up against the crisscross of the dog's cage. Old man was probably lying down.

On his trip back from the van, the trooper said, "Looks like you're on your own, Alex. You be sure to drive safely." He went around back and slammed the trunk.

Alex lowered himself into the driver's seat, momentarily forgetting how to start the engine. He may have even forgotten how to drive, and he wasn't about to put himself under the scrutiny of the mighty trooper. So he grabbed a map and waited it out.

The van pulled away first. The trooper followed.

Alex was alone, still in shock. There were actually two shocks mixed together. First was Lester's arrest, which was partially Alex's fault. The second was that no one among that brain trust of law enforcement had bothered to check his license.

Until now, he had been too nervous to consider what to do next. The only certainty was that he couldn't just sit there. Another cop would come—a savvier cop—who would gladly arrest him for unlawful use of a motorized vehicle. He started the engine and brought the Cadillac to traffic speed. He was officially breaking the law. The map of the Southeastern States lay on the passenger seat. It would be simple enough to follow the yellow highlighted route all the way up to New York. That's what Lester had told him to do. Alex could keep his speed down and even drive through the night.

Meanwhile, Lester would be wasting away in some jail cell. Nothing could be more depressing, maybe not even death.

Alex pulled into a rest area and studied the map. Brunswick was way over on the opposite corner of the state, about as far as you could travel and still be in Georgia. And there was no direct route. But a germinating feeling told him he could make it. He could continue north until he reached the southern outskirts of Atlanta, go southeast on I-75 then due east on I-16 all the way to Savannah. For the last leg, he'd take I-95 south to Brunswick.

But before any of that he needed snacks, and he needed a bathroom. He found an open stall and let out a nerve-wracked storm of gas and diarrhea. When he was all done, he felt renewed. As if here, in this very time and location, was the passing of the Old Alex and the start of a new one. And this New Alex saw himself as responsible. People could count on him to do what was right. Getting Lester out of jail would be his first big mission.

At the vending machines he realized how little there was for the newly health-conscious. But he had to get something. For a total of eight dollars, he purchased a bottle of Gatorade, a bottle of water, two bags of trail mix and a granola bar. He plopped the items into the center console and started the engine.

THE ROUTE was simple enough, but the map hadn't warned him that he was about to be bogged down by heavy traffic and a disorienting tangle of on and off ramps. He wasn't even going into Atlanta, just the outer suburbs by the airport. Which proved to be interstate mayhem. As traffic slowed to a standstill, he cursed his navigational stupidity.

He thought of the congestion-free trip from Albany to Fort Lauderdale and how Lester had smartly routed them away from major cities. By taking I-81 instead of I-95, they had missed all of Metro New York, Philadelphia, Baltimore and Washington, DC. If those cities were anything like Atlanta, the trip would have taken a week.

There was only half a mile before his exit and three lanes to cut across, but traffic had settled into walking speed, and the gaps between vehicles were almost nonexistent. A golf cart might squeeze through, not a Cadillac Deville. He flipped on his blinker, as if that mattered. In the midst of this mess, a passenger jet shot across his visual field—so close he could count the five lines on the US Airways logo flag.

Normally, in a situation like this, he would have imagined his father stepping in with navigational guidance. As Alex lunged into the space between two tractor trailers, he might've been tempted to bring his father in on the maneuver. The man's skillful eyes would see the road through Alex's eyes...and so on.

But the game lost its appeal on the day Alex met his father in the flesh. "It was stupid anyway," he said to the truck in front of him. "I did all those things on my own. You were never there. Never!"

Something about talking out loud in the air-tight cabin of the car felt gratifying. Besides, it was practically his car. He could do whatever the hell he wanted. And he wanted to talk. Specifically, he wanted to talk to his father. "You son of a bitch," he said. The words felt raw and true.

"You could've picked up the damn phone, you chicken shit. You could have visited too. But no, not you. You were too scared. You were too ashamed. You were too caught up in your own little life. You barely moved a muscle for me, except to write some letters...which I never got!"

At this point, he could have easily turned the anger toward his mother. But he decided to keep them separate—one battle at a time.

There must have been a dozen or so cars passing in the left lane. Some people looked at him, but Alex kept talking as if there was a Bluetooth in his ear. That was one of the great things about modern technology—you could talk to yourself and not appear crazy.

He felt an easing of stress as he broke away from the gridlock. Metro Atlanta faded into a bad memory. He went back to slamming his father. "I hope you made a big fancy breakfast," he said. "I hope you waited and waited for me. I hope you stared at your diamond-studded watch and waited."

A new feeling emerged unexpectedly from under the anger.

"You waited, just like I always waited." It was too much to contain. "And I didn't show up, just like you never showed up." Tears streamed down his face.

"I hope you missed me," he managed to say. Then his final words of truth: "Because I missed you."

It occurred to him that it didn't really matter that his father was gay. What mattered was the same thing that had always mattered. For all those years, the man was never there.

CHAPTER TWENTY-ONE

He had driven over seven hours, never budging beyond the posted speed limit, even though nearly every other vehicle on the road went faster. He wasn't about to put himself at risk just to gain time. A billboard for the Brunswick Days Inn featured the word *pool* in its description. As he turned onto the Island Parkway in the direction of downtown, he visualized himself swimming among a throng of bikini-clad beauties, and that was all it took to sway him.

He turned off at Gloucester Street, and the motel was right there. He figured a hundred should cover it, so he locked the rest of the money in the glove box and made his way to the lobby.

A man behind the counter was talking on the phone. He had curly hair that was moussed in a meticulous way, and he wore a necktie showcasing a variety of sailboats. The man raised his chin toward Alex and whispered, "Just a minute."

Alex felt for his wallet and checked to make sure his keys hadn't fallen out of his pocket. The clerk hung up the phone. "Can I help you?"

"Yeah," Alex said, "I'd like a room overlooking the pool, non-smoking."

"Is it just for you?"

"Yeah, just me."

"How many nights will you be staying with us?"

Alex felt as if he'd been thrown a trick question. It was Thursday, just after seven—no chance of getting started until tomorrow. If he couldn't handle the situation in one day, he'd have to push it to next week. But he didn't want to think about that. The clerk was waiting, fiddling with his fingers as if to exaggerate the delay. "I don't really know, maybe two, maybe three."

"Well, why don't we say three? That way, we won't give up your room if you need it. If you leave before then, just be sure to cancel any remaining nights or you'll be charged." He smiled brightly. "You wouldn't want that."

"Good point," Alex said.

The clerk pecked away at his keyboard then asked, "You here for business or pleasure?"

Alex didn't know what to say. He couldn't categorize it as either, but he had to say something. "Sort of business, I guess."

"Company name?"

"Uh, there's really no company. It's more like an important errand I've got to do."

The clerk toned down his smile. "If what you're planning on doing is illegal, we want no part of it here. I'm sorry, but you'll have to find lodging elsewhere."

"No, it's not illegal, I swear."

"Well, then," the man crossed his arms over his nautical tie, "mind telling me what it is?"

Alex hesitated for a moment. What kind of desk clerk probes into your personal business? It had to be a violation of motel etiquette.

But as long as Alex got a room in the end, he didn't mind talking. In fact, after all the hours on the road, it felt good to speak with another human being. "It's my friend, Lester. I've gotta get him out of jail."

"I see," the clerk said, raising one eyebrow above the other. His face was open-book expressive. "And why does this Lester deserve to be sprung from jail?"

Alex's response came without censor. "Because what he did was noble."

"And how, may I ask, did Lester earn such nobility?"

Alex looked around the lobby. There wasn't anybody else around. "All right," he said, "he hit a cop who was bad. He did it to protect me."

"Now this is getting interesting." The clerk leaned forward against the counter. "Protect you from what?"

Alex explained about the cop's girlfriend and that he hadn't known the man was a cop. He gave the lobby another quick scan. "The guy came out of nowhere and told me to move. I sort of stalled, I guess, so he shoved a peach cobbler in my face and called me a nigger lover."

The clerk gave a look of disgust.

"That's when Lester stepped in and whacked the guy with a stick."

"Hooray for Lester," shouted the clerk. "Your story makes sense. I just might have to find you a room." He punched a few keys. "How does fifty-two dollars a night sound?"

"That's fine."

"And how will you be paying?"

"Cash." Alex opened his wallet. "I got a hundred dollar bill right here."

"Figures," the clerk said, rolling his eyes. "We'll need a credit card to handle any incidental charges, should they occur."

"No," Alex said. "I mean...I don't have a credit card."

The clerk shook his head and said, "Figures." Then he looked out the lobby window. "Is that your Cadillac?"

"Yeah, I got it from Lester."

The clerk raised both hands. "Maybe you shouldn't tell me anything more."

"What about the room?"

There was a spell of silence. Alex's hands were cold. He stuffed them into his pockets.

"Listen," the clerk said, "I'm putting my job on the line here. So you better be honorable. Pay me for three nights, straight up cash. Don't break anything in the room, don't steal any towels or anything else, and come here to use the phone." He ran a key card through a slot. "My name's Dale. I work two to ten. You need something, come to me."

"Thanks," Alex said, "I've got the rest of the money in the car."

Dale rolled his eyes again and said, "Figures."

AS PROMISED, Alex's room was on the second floor overlooking the pool. But there was nothing but pale blue water, certainly no babes in bikinis. He opened the door and set his duffel bag on the king bed. Secured under his left arm was Selma's gift. He couldn't wait any longer. Now felt like the appropriate time.

He placed the rectangular box on the table and examined it for the first time. The purple matte wrapping paper had a couple of ripples on top, which must have been the police dog's dried slobber. But it was still beautiful. A golden bow secured a little card. He tore it open and read:

> *Dear Alexander the Great,*
>
> *Keep running after all your dreams. Love, Selma*

He set aside the card and knew immediately what was inside the box—the only question was style and fit. He opened it. They were blue Nike Shox Turbos with spider web stripes and black swooshes. He checked the tongue: size twelve. She had done her research.

His heart felt big and warm as he laced up the new running shoes and slid them on. He hopped around the room to check the fit. They were perfect, could have been custom made for him. He'd have to find a place to give them a proper initiation.

He returned to the lobby and asked Dale about a good place to run.

"Use the track at Coffin Park," Dale said, pointing out the window.

"That sounds morbid," Alex said. Lester would have loved it.

"It's not like that. You'll be fine. But don't stay after dark." He went on to state the park's policy of closing at dusk because that's when drug dealers came out and the cops made their raids. He finished with a sharp-eyed stare. "Follow my advice or you may end up joining your friend."

Alex ran weightlessly across the street and down the road that took him to the trail. He stopped and stretched at the entrance, checked the location of the setting sun and worked his way into a good pace.

NEXT MORNING, when he woke up much later than he wanted, he noticed an envelope at the threshold of the door. The return address was the Days Inn, but smack in the center was his name written in neat penmanship. He tore it open. The inside note had the same style writing. It was from Dale, instructing Alex that he would probably need a bail bondsman if he hoped to spring Lester. And Dale knew just the person. The note gave the bondsman's name and driving directions to his office.

CHAPTER TWENTY-TWO

There were no available parking spots at the Freedom Bonds storefront, so he parked the Cadillac next door, facing an old thrift shop called Another Man's Treasure. It should've been called *One Man's Junk*. There were aluminum pots and pans on display, hub caps and television sets that looked like they'd come from the days of pre-cable. Alex got out of the car and double-checked the locks.

He expected a crowd at Freedom Bonds, but when he pulled open the door to the clanging of bells there was no one inside. A moment later, he could hear ambiguous sounds, a toilet flush and then running water. Out came a stocky black man with a rolled-up magazine in his hand. He limped forward, causing Alex to look at the man's elaborate knee brace.

"Appreciate your patience," the man said as he sat behind a desk. "Nothing gets in the way of my morning constitutional. My wife says she could set the clocks to'em. And sometimes she calls, right in the middle, just to piss me off. Have a seat."

Alex smiled as he lowered himself into a chair. It was a total TMI situation, but he didn't mind. In fact, the story helped ease his nerves. He leaned forward and said, "I'm Alex. I was told by Dale at the Days Inn you could help."

The man shook Alex's hand and said, "Clyde Simms. I haven't seen Dale Beekman in a couple of years. How's he doing?"

"Fine, I guess," Alex said. "He wears flashy ties."

"That's Dale—swings the other way, but a heck of a good guy. He and I went to high school together."

Again, Alex had missed the sexual orientation cues, making him feel like an idiot all over again. It was possible that Clyde took Alex to be gay by association. So to help bolster his case, Alex said, "You look like Bo Jackson," which in a way Clyde did.

"Ha!" Clyde said. "You trying to butter me up."

"No, really."

"Well, truth is, I played DT at Georgia." He locked his hands over his chest and leaned back. "All-SEC two years in a row."

Alex had no idea what the man was talking about, but knew enough to be mightily impressed. "Wow," he said. "That's awesome."

"It was a lot of fun until I damn near split my knee apart playing up at Syracuse. There was a seam in that ridiculous Astroturf, I tell you." He reached down toward the hardware surrounding his right knee. "I'll live with that till the day I die."

"That totally sucks," Alex said, considering this enough bad karma to scratch Syracuse off his list of college options.

Clyde leaned forward over his desk. "So tell me, what brings you here?"

Alex explained that he and Lester, an elderly black man, had been traveling from Albany and stopped in Brunswick. Then he gave full account of Lester's offense at the truck stop and of his own involvement. He told how Lester was taken away in a K-9 van and was now incarcerated here. He finished by saying, "I can't let him stay in jail. I've gotta get him out."

Clyde took a couple of notes then said, "First thing you'll need to do is go to the county courthouse and see the clerk. If Lester's as old as you say, he'll get a more expedient hearing. They might even lump his arraignment in with his bail hearing. If he came in yesterday, he could see the judge as early as today. Whenever it is, get there on time. It'll be quick."

Alex gave a half-understanding nod.

"If they set bail, we're in business. The bond to spring him is fifteen percent. Since Lester's from New York, there's also a five hundred dollar out-of-state fee. If he's held without bail, we're screwed." Clyde tore out the sheet of paper he'd been writing on. "Let me know how it goes." Then he explained where the courthouse was, and he handed Alex a business card.

"Thanks," Alex said. On his way out he looked at Clyde's card, which made him smile. There were the words: **FREEDOM BONDS** in boldface. Just below, it said, *Not your average oxymoron*. He stuffed the card into his pocket and walked the four blocks to the county courthouse.

The brick building was centered on a square of lawn filled with bushes and moss-draped trees. The inside entrance featured a security checkpoint. A uniformed guard asked Alex where he was headed. Figuring there was no reason to lie, Alex said, "I need to find out when my friend sees the judge."

The guard pointed to a windowed office. "Pam will take care of you."

A line of three people stood in front of Alex, which gave him time to settle his nerves and frame his question. The woman they were all waiting to see had a high-pitched Southern voice, blonde pageboy haircut and perhaps the biggest set of breasts Alex had ever seen. Her cleavage, from what he could see of it, was longer than most butt cracks. His first thought was that she could store a sandwich under those things and forget it was there. His second thought smacked of an entirely new philosophy—it was that some breasts were actually too big.

He was next in line and could now read her name badge: *Pamela Blizzard* in fancy italics. Then it was his turn. She said, "What can I do for you, hon?"

Alex stepped forward. "I need to find out when my friend gets arraigned." The word *arraigned* sounded sophisticated coming out of his sixteen-year-old mouth, and it took his mind away from Pamela's breasts.

"What's your friend's name?" She looked down at a computer monitor.

"Lester Bray. He was brought to jail yesterday."

"Name sounds familiar." She clicked her mouse. "Isn't he that old man who hit Randy Burgess at Mega Fuel?"

"Sounds right," Alex said. The whole scene at the truck stop flashed before him.

Pamela softened her voice. "Between you and me, Randy's an awful man, dates a friend of mine, treats her just awful. I was actually glad to hear he'd been hurt."

"It was my fault," Alex said. "I started it."

"Well, I'm sure he did something to get you riled up." She smiled at Alex then looked back at her screen.

Just like that, he got an erection. It occurred to him that Pamela's breasts might not be too big after all. "I found it," she said. "You better hurry. Started five minutes ago." She placed a floor-plan on the counter and pointed. "Right here, Courtroom Four."

ALEX FELT like a sinner late for church as he entered the courtroom while the judge was speaking. He slid into the back row—twenty or so feet directly behind Lester and his lawyer.

Randy Burgess, in full cop regalia, sat on the other side. He was smiling and whispering something into his attorney's ear.

"Mr. Bray," the elderly judge said. "You've been charged with third degree aggravated battery. How do you plead?"

Lester's attorney said, "We plead no contest, Your Honor, with full intention of counsel."

The judge looked directly at Lester. "Are you aware, Mr. Bray, that a plea of no contest gives up your right to trial?"

"I am," Lester said.

"Are you aware that your record will show a conviction?"

"I'm aware."

"Mr. Bray," the judge went on, "have you been coerced in any way to enter this plea?"

"No, Your Honor, I've decided to go along."

"Do you wish to say anything to the court before we proceed?"

Lester looked over at Randy Burgess, scowled for a moment and then said, "No, Your Honor, I'll pass."

The judge pointed toward both lawyers and said, "I'll speak with you two." The three men exited through a door behind the witness stand.

Alex focused on the back of Lester's head, wondering if the old man's ears had always been so big. But then he remembered from biology class that ears were cartilage, and cartilage—unlike the rest of your body—kept growing until you died. Lester's head was downcast. If Alex hadn't known better, he would have thought the old man was praying.

Then Alex looked over at Randy Burgess who was staring straight back and smiling. It was the kind of smile that attracted itself to blood. Suddenly, Alex felt like he should be the one praying. He looked down and closed his eyes.

The judge resumed his bench while the lawyers returned to their clients.

"Mr. Bray," the judge said, "this court accepts your plea of no contest for the charge of third degree aggravated battery. I've heard from you, your attorney and the prosecution, and I've given close consideration to the facts of this case." He put on a pair of low-slung glasses and looked down at a sheet of paper. "I hereby sentence you to thirty days incarceration, or ninety hours community service. You'll be required to take part in an anger management class, and you'll pay a fine of $2,000." He looked straight at Lester. "Do you understand the terms of this sentence?"

"I do," Lester said. The words came out flat.

"Good," the judge said. "Since you're from out of state and therefore a flight risk, your release is contingent upon you paying the fine. Furthermore, if you elect community service, you've got seven days to meet with your probation officer." He picked up his gavel. "This court is adjourned."

Alex felt winded even though he hadn't done anything. He remained seated while everyone else got up. There was a sliver of

Lester between two men who helped him out of his chair. Then Randy Burgess came strutting up the aisle. He had stitches angled across the length of his left temple.

He looked down at Alex and said, "Watch your step, pervert."

CHAPTER TWENTY-THREE

Alex's return walk to Freedom Bonds was bogged down by the fear of Randy Burgess and the complexities of the judge's sentence. Even if he had the money to pay the fine, Lester would still need to stay in Georgia, see a probation officer, take a class and do a stint of community service. The whole thing felt overwhelming.

He opened the door and entered the office. There sat Clyde at his desk, hovering over a half-eaten sub. He dabbed his mouth with a napkin and said, "Alex, have a seat. You hungry?"

"No, I'm fine."

"You gotta be hungry." Clyde reached for an additional sandwich. "Here, this is good. You'll be doing me a favor." He explained that it was a pork chop sandwich from Willie's and that his wife always brought him two, which was one too many if he ever hoped to shed pounds. He placed the thing on a section of newspaper and ushered it forward. "You'll like it, long as you're not a vegetarian."

"Thanks," Alex said. He felt unworthy of the kind gesture and was afraid of not liking the sub.

"So how'd it go?" Clyde asked.

"Not so good. Lester pled no contest, and the judge gave him thirty days in jail or ninety hours community service. He has to pay a fine of $2,000. And since he's not from Georgia, they won't let him out until he pays. Plus, he has to take an anger management class."

"Your friend must've made quite an impression," Clyde said. "Or he had one shitty lawyer."

Alex took his first bite of sandwich. It was packed with chunks of spicy pork, mustard and sautéed onions. He chewed it down to the point where he could speak. "I don't know where I'll get $2,000." He chewed a little more—incredibly tasty. "But I've gotta find a way."

"That's what friends do." Clyde ate his last bite, balled his food wrap and napkin into a tight clump and sky-hooked it ten feet into a wastebasket. "Listen, Alex, there's no bail, so you don't need me anymore. But I'll make it easy. You get whoever's gonna pay the fine to call me. That could be Lester himself, if he has the money."

Given the way Lester had talked about his financial situation, he could have easily paid the fine. But Alex hadn't come all this way to take the easy road. He needed to carry part of the burden. He said, "I can't let him pay."

"So you'll find someone. Have that person call me. I'll take care of it from there. Assuming Lester would rather not spend a month in jail, I'll contact you at the motel when he's ready to go."

"Sounds easy when you put it like that," Alex said. Finding someone to fork over that kind of money was anything but easy. But he wanted to stay positive. After he finished the sandwich, he thanked Clyde and said, "Hope I can find someone."

"You will. Just put some thought into it."

ALEX'S NERVOUS system was nearly maxed out as he drove the

straight line to the motel. At every intersection and with every stray noise, his brain conjured images of raging Randy Burgess in a squad car.

Finally, he was able to pull into the motel parking lot without police accompaniment. It was just after two o'clock. Dale would be on duty. He deserved thanks for his help.

Just like the previous day, Dale was on the phone. He held up a finger and smiled. Today's tie was an array of colorful balloons—the kind you'd see at a kid's birthday party. He hung up and said, "Well if it isn't Noble Alex, back from his day's errands."

Although he liked the moniker better than Alexander the Great, he still wasn't worthy of it. "I'm not the noble one," he said.

"Details," Dale said. "You're pretty noble."

"Actually, I came in to thank you for the note. I sat down with Clyde and got some good information."

"Glad he could help. Clyde is wonderful. Poor man had a career waiting for him in the NFL."

"I saw his knee-brace," Alex said.

Dale pushed aside his keyboard and sat in its place. "So what's next for Noble Alex?"

"I don't know. I've got to find someone who's willing to pay $2,000 to get Lester out. That won't be easy."

"Hmm, that is asking quite a lot of someone." Dale caressed his chin. "If you're thinking of asking me, you can march yourself right out of here."

"No," Alex said, "I'd never ask that." It occurred to him that he was having a perfectly respectable conversation with a gay man. And it didn't bother him. In fact, he was pleased with himself.

"You look like you just swallowed a fly," Dale said. "What's on your mind?"

"Nothing really."

"Go on, what is it?"

"It's just this weird thought I had." Alex looked down at a crescent stain in the carpet, like someone had left a leaking bucket of battleship gray paint. He mustered the courage to speak. "I was wondering if you thought you'd make a good father."

Dale made a kind of whiplash maneuver. "Now that's an interesting question! Good Lord, you surprise me." He arched a bit forward. "You know how rare it is to get asked a question like that?"

"I was just wondering."

"No, really," Dale said. "Most folks ask about the weather." He looked back at the clock on the wall. "By the way, we're expecting a hell of a storm in about thirty minutes. Or they ask for directions or extra towels. But you come in here with a question like that. I'm telling you—"

"You don't have to answer."

"Actually, I will," Dale said. "In fact, this is something that's been on my mind. I'm not getting any younger, and neither is Chip, my partner. We've been thinking about having a couple of foster kids in the house and then maybe adopting one of them."

Alex put the two names together and chuckled.

"All right," Dale said, "laugh it up. His real name's Charles, but ever since we've been together, it's been Chip. If I had a dollar for every Chip and Dale joke." He crossed his arms over a cluster of balloons. "Well, I wouldn't be working in this place, that's for sure."

"I didn't mean to laugh."

Dale smirked and said, "Back to your question. Yes, in fact, I think I'd make a good father." His face turned dreamy. "There's so much compassion and knowledge inside me that I've never been able to share. I could share that with a child on a daily basis. I'd make sure he or she grew up to be something special. That's what I think."

As Alex listened to these words, he imagined a barometer of truth registering the full hundred percent. "I hope you get the opportunity." It was all he could think to say.

"Now I've got something to ask you, Noble Alex." His face wasn't dreamy anymore—it looked baffled. "What on earth would lead you to ask such a question?"

"I'm not sure."

"Utter bullshit." Dale was scowling. "There's a reason for everything. I'm willing to bet you know exactly what it is."

Alex's face felt like a barbecue grill. "Okay," he said, swallowing his nerves. "The thing is, my father's gay."

"Hmm," Dale said. "I knew there was something about you."

"When I found out, I hated him for it. I left town, haven't seen him since."

"That's not an unusual reaction. For two years, my parents didn't speak to me. So don't beat yourself up."

"Yeah," Alex said, "but he was never there, even before I found out. He left when I was a year old. I was the one who hunted him down."

"Now that sounds like a reason to hate him," Dale said. "I'm sure I'd feel the same way."

"I don't think I really hate him, at least not anymore."

"Your dad made a bad choice. If he's got a conscience, I'm sure he's suffering right about now."

"So why am I the one who feels bad? I stood him up for breakfast and just split town."

"You feel bad because you've got a conscience."

A family of three entered the lobby, but Dale kept talking. "Forgive yourself," he said, far too loudly. "In time, maybe you'll be able to forgive your dad." Then he looked at the two parents and said, "May I help you?"

Hearing advice like this in front of strangers was totally embarrassing. Alex slunk back and sat in the middle of a lumpy couch. Dale seemed to have questionable boundaries when it came to dealing with people, but his advice was pretty solid. He checked the family into a non-smoking room with two queen beds and told them the best place to park. Each of the parents took a key, and they were gone.

Alex returned to the counter. "I've been thinking about what you said."

Dale was at the computer. "Good," he said. "You keep it in mind until it doesn't mean anything." He stepped away from the screen. "So what does your father do for a living?"

"He owns a restaurant down in Fort Lauderdale. I think he's pretty rich. He lives right on the ocean."

"Mercy," Dale said. "I think you've got your answer."

"What answer?"

As if to check for blindness, Dale waved a hand in front of Alex. "*Hello*," he said, "seems like two grand wouldn't be much of a stretch for your dad."

"Yeah, but I couldn't ask him for that."

"Why not? He's your father. That's the kind of thing a father does for his son."

"Yeah, but he doesn't even know Lester."

"Yeah, but, yeah, but, yeah, but...." Dale's voice was a playful melody. "You're full of excuses." He pointed a finger. "I think you're scared."

It was true. Alex was petrified at the thought of calling his father for such a weighty favor. Dale pressed on. "What are you afraid of?"

"I don't know. It's a lot to ask."

"You're right about that. But if my calculations are accurate, he owes you. Fact, he owes you big. Let this be an opportunity for him to start leveling the scale."

"I don't think he owes me," Alex said.

"It's honorable of you to say that. You're not a spoiled brat. But when a man fathers a child, it's his duty to raise that child the best he can. Your dad failed all these years. Two thousand dollars is nothing compared to that."

This whole line of reasoning was altogether foreign to Alex. He said, "I hadn't thought about it like that."

"Well, you better think of something, while your friend sits in jail."

"Okay," Alex said, not sure whether he meant it.

"Tell you what, you call him right back there." Dale pointed to the little office behind him. "Dial direct. I'll cover it."

Alex's anxiety jumped into a new orbit. "I should think about what to say."

"Right, you keep thinking." Dale shook his head slowly. "You happen to know the statistics on jailhouse violence?"

The mere suggestion of danger caused him to picture frail old Lester, minus his protective stick, fending off a pack of gangbangers, pimps, drug addicts and sexual predators. "All right," Alex said, retrieving the card with his father's cell number and Clyde's business card.

"Go back there and sit down. Don't even think about it. Just dial the number."

This was perhaps the most terrifying thing Alex had ever done, worse than having his twelve-year molars yanked out. But why was it so scary? He picked up the phone and pressed the sequence of digits.

There was a ring...a second...then a third. No one was there. The prospect of leaving a message instead of actually having a conversation was liberating, and it helped lessen the fear. The greeting said, "Hi, you've reached the private line of Scott Riley. I'm not available right now. Leave a message. Thanks."

Alex cleared his throat and said, "Hello dad, it's me, Alex." He cleared his throat again. "I'm calling to ask for a really big favor." Pause. "It's my friend Lester. He's in jail, and it's my fault." Pause. "I've gotta get him out, but I don't have the money." Pause. "I was hoping you could come up with it." He went on to give Clyde's name and phone number. He ended the message by saying, "Thanks a bunch, dad," just in case his father actually came through.

He hung up the phone.

"That was pretty good," Dale said. He'd been standing at the door listening the whole time. "Now we'll see what he does."

"I was so nervous," Alex said.

"Perfectly understandable."

"Yeah, but why?"

"Because you just put yourself at risk for more rejection." He poked a finger at Alex's chest. "And that, Noble Alex, is one of the hardest things there is to do."

A new feeling crept over him. It was sadness, and it ran the risk of turning to tears. He got up from the desk and made his way out of the office. From the other side of the counter, he said, "Clyde knows to call here if anything happens."

"Good," Dale said. "Soon as he calls, I'll transfer him to your room."

"Thanks a lot." Alex knew there was something more he wanted to say. And he knew exactly what it was. He sniffed hard and forced himself to look at Dale.

"You'd make an excellent father."

CHAPTER TWENTY-FOUR

He had planned to go for another run at Coffin Park, but when he looked out his motel window there were branches of palmetto trees blowing sideways and the first gusts of rain speckling the pool. A flash of lightning pulsated to the east. Dale had been right about the weather. So he turned on the television and channel-surfed from one program to another. There was nothing to watch, and he didn't feel like drawing. He fast-forwarded through a dozen songs on his iPod. None of them held his attention. He shut it off, preferring the violent sounds of the storm.

He got down on the carpeted floor and sped through a series of push-ups. He managed twenty, pressed on to twenty-five before converting to girl-style then finally collapsing. He repeated the cycle four times, managing only eight reps by the final excruciating set. His arms and chest were throbbing.

He spread a towel on the floor and did stomach crunches, imagining all the while bands of muscle complimenting the heft of his chest. Next came jumping jacks, which looked ridiculous no matter how buff you were. So he closed the curtains and turned on all the lights. He jumped and counted in rhythm, sweat flying off of him. The percussive noise would have been annoying if someone occupied the room below, and that complaint would come back to him via Dale. It was enough to make him stop.

The noise of rain and wind and thunder filled the room. The scale of it was enormous. Yet he was protected from it all, nestled in a cocoon of comfort and safety. It made him feel humble and small.

He looked at the clock—just after five, and it was Friday. Which meant no more leniencies from his mother. If she was ever to call the authorities, now would be the time. And there would be no more second chances for Lester with Rebecca and Elder Spring. More immediately, Clyde had probably left his office and wouldn't return until Monday. Even though the motel room felt comfortable now, two more days of waiting loomed like a purgatory of boredom. He opened the curtains and checked the sky. The rain was still thrashing. If he didn't hear from Clyde soon, he'd go downstairs and ask Dale if he could use the phone. He'd call the jail for visiting hours.

THE RINGING phone was like a defibrillator at his chest. He ran over and grabbed it in the middle of the second ring. He tried to say the word *hello* in a cool nonchalant way, like he'd been handling important business all day, and here was just another call. But his voice broke with an embarrassing chirp.

"Hey, Alex, it's Clyde. We got mostly good news and a little bad."

"Really?"

"Good news is, your father came through, wired the money as soon as he got word."

"That's great." Alex pictured his dad rushing to the bank on his behalf. It was the exact opposite of being ignored. "What's the bad news?"

"We missed the deadline for today. You'll have to pick up Lester tomorrow. Be there at nine o'clock sharp."

"Hope he can handle one more night."

"Nothing to worry about," Clyde said. "You've done a good job."

As Alex hung up the phone, he felt a true sense of achievement. He had actually pulled it off. Soon he'd have to thank his father, but not now. He sprang to his feet and began dancing, not caring if people were to walk by and stare. It was his victory dance. He looked down at his sneakers, which reminded him of a different kind of joy. It occurred to him that life had a variety of joys to offer. Each came with its own color, like the balloons on Dale's tie. But you didn't have to wait for your birthday. That was the best part. You could feel this way anytime.

NEXT MORNING, Alex counted seventeen blocks from motel to county jail. The first blocks were the most nerve-wracking, filled once again with visions of Randy Burgess and handcuffs and a flatbed tow-truck hauling away the Cadillac. He should've taken a cab.

By the time he got to Norwich Street, his nerves had settled to a manageable level. He parked the car near the jail entry. The time was 8:55. He entered a no-frills reception area, turned left past a gumball machine and stood before a Plexiglas window.

A uniformed woman sat behind a counter. "Can I help you?"

"I'm here to pick up Lester Bray."

"I'll need to see your ID," she said.

While she examined his permit, he looked back at the Cadillac staring right at them. *God, I'm an idiot*, he thought. But then she returned the card without comment. She pressed her intercom and announced, "Lester Bray, three-green," whatever that meant. Then she looked at Alex and said, "Have a seat."

A tattered copy of *The Brunswick News* was spread across two chairs. He organized the mess and read the front page headlines followed by the weather—hot, sunny and humid. He had been thinking of getting a job down here while Lester served out his stint of community service, so he flipped to the classifieds. There wasn't much available, and almost everything required a high school diploma or at least a GED. But there was an ad for a dishwasher and another for a janitor's helper, and neither required anything beyond capable limbs. At the risk of getting chastised by the receptionist, he turned away and tore out the area with the two ads and stuffed it into his pocket.

A distant metal door opened and clanked shut. Then another door much closer in proximity. He stood up and realized he was afraid. He knew that jail changed people, usually not for the better. Maybe the Lester he saw two days ago wouldn't be the same person now. The door opened, and out came a female guard carrying Lester's old suitcase.

"Right here," Alex said.

The guard said, "He's slow, but he's coming." She set the bag next to Alex.

And then it sounded like someone was running a marathon with a snorkel.

Lester entered the waiting room and turned to Alex. "My God!" he said, gasping. There was a bandage wrapped around his right wrist, but otherwise he looked the same.

"Hey, Lester."

"My God," the old man repeated. "How on earth did you manage this?"

"I got help," Alex said, "lots of it."

"Give me your hand."

Alex put a trembling hand forward and said, "I'm happy to see you."

Lester placed both hands around Alex's, pulled him close and said, "Happy to see you too, kid."

"I'm sorry," Alex said.

"For what?"

"For getting you into this mess."

Lester steadied himself against the back of a chair. "Got myself into it. You got nothing to be sorry about. Fact, you ought to be proud."

Alex couldn't help but smile. "I am a little proud."

"Good," Lester said. "Let's talk about it over breakfast. You're driving, and you're buying."

Alex lifted the bulky Samsonite and steadied Lester while simultaneously carrying the suitcase to the Cadillac. "What happened there?" Alex was pointing to the bandage on Lester's wrist. He started the engine and turned up the AC.

"Had to wear a damn cuff all the way down here—took quite a toll on my ancient skin."

Alex nodded and said, "So where to?"

"Let's go back to that truck stop where all this foolishness started."

Alex had thought his anxiety was done for the day, but it flickered back. "You sure you want to go there?"

"I am, and I want my stick."

Alex pulled away from the parking lot. "It's behind the seat, where you left it."

"Good, I been missing that stick. Of course I've been missing you too."

"Same here," Alex said. "It's been a weird couple of days."

"You're telling me." Lester shook his head. "So how'd you get the money?"

"That's the amazing thing. It was my dad."

"Ain't that something...what made you think to ask him?"

"I've met some good people here." Alex went on to recount almost everything that had happened over the past two days. He began with his cross-state drive, his tirade against his father and then Dale at the Days Inn. He talked about Clyde at the oxymoronic Freedom Bonds and the enormous breasts of Pamela Blizzard. Then he returned to Dale and finished by way of saying, "I'm trying to learn about forgiveness."

"Indeed you are," Lester said. "Almost makes this whole thing worthwhile." The Mega Fuel truck stop was just ahead. "Let's call this our celebration breakfast, kid."

Alex liked the way that sounded. His only request was that they not sit at the same table. "Anywhere but there," he said.

"Fine, we'll get a booth."

Alex put the stick in Lester's hand while scanning the parking lot for signs of Randy Burgess. "Hope he's not here," he said.

"Wouldn't matter if he was," Lester said. "We won't cause any trouble."

There were a variety of open booths in the restaurant, but Lester walked directly to the one in the corner—same booth Randy's girlfriend had occupied with her voluptuous cleavage on display. That was the only good memory Alex had of the place.

The same skinny waitress with the same acne-ravaged complexion approached the booth with menus. "What can I get y'all to drink?"

She had the same Southern twang, but it sounded sweeter than it had eight days earlier.

"Do you remember us, sweetheart?" Lester asked.

She looked at Lester, then at Alex and said, "By God, I do." Her eyes shifted back to Lester. "You found yourself a heap of trouble here. Hope you found a way out."

"We did," Lester said. "We came back to enjoy ourselves this time, and do right by you...give you a nice tip for helping us out."

She smiled and said, "You don't have to do that. I was glad to help."

"Makes three of us," Lester said. "How fresh is your coffee? Last two days, I've had nothing but jail swill."

"I'll make sure it's a fresh pot."

They agreed on the breakfast buffet, and it was gratifying to watch Lester take one contented bite after another. "Food at the jail looked edible enough," Lester said between bites. "But no matter what it was—eggs, grits or toast—it all tasted exactly the same."

"Sounds wonderful," Alex said as he pulled the torn newsprint out of his pocket. "I was thinking of getting a job down here."

Lester brought his coffee mug to his mouth then set it down without taking a sip. "Now why in the hell would you do that?"

"Because you've got that class and community service. I'll stay here to keep you company."

"That's nice, kid—real nice—but the answer's no."

"Why? I can wash dishes." He pointed to the ad. "And I'd help pay the rent."

"Just hearing you make the offer is good enough for me."

"I can totally do it," Alex said.

Lester gave a momentary stare, like that was enough to settle the matter. Then he went back to eating and reflecting on how good the food was compared to the slop he'd been served in jail. "It's good to experience some lack in your life," he said, "makes you more appreciative."

"Why can't you let me help?"

"Listen, kid, your life's up in New York. And your mother would like nothing more than to chop off my head right about now."

"She doesn't know where we are."

"Doesn't matter." He pointed his fork at the scrap of newsprint. "That's not part of the plan."

"Plans change. I want to stay here and work."

The waitress came back with a steaming pot of coffee. "How's everything? Can I filler up?"

"Everything's great," Lester said, putting a hand over his mug. "No more for me."

"I got a question," Alex said to the waitress, "do you need a dishwasher here?"

"Don't mind him," Lester said. "Kid's been acting strange this morning."

"I can look into it," the waitress said.

"Don't bother," Lester said. "We'll just take the check when you're ready."

She set the tab on the table. "Y'all come back and see me again."

Lester watched the waitress move on to other customers. Then he spoke softly. "I got no intention of staying here. We're getting you settled back into your house. That's what we're doing."

Alex knew enough to keep his voice at a whisper. "What about your probation?"

"If they care enough to track me down, I'll get a goddamn lawyer in New York." He raised his napkin to his mouth. "Get the sentence commuted."

"When do you want to leave?"

"You still got some of that money I gave you?"

"Yeah," Alex said, "most of it."

Lester tapped the table. "Put down fifty bucks, and we leave right now."

CHAPTER TWENTY-FIVE

Lester had insisted on driving, saying he felt bloated from overeating and wanted to take his mind off the discomfort. As they rounded the northbound ramp onto I-95, he said, "Simplest things are the hardest to manage."

Alex wondered how long it would take the old man to come around to the topic of death.

"Breathing, sleeping, eating," Lester went on, "doesn't get much simpler than that. But those are the things that get you...right up to the end."

Bingo—less than five minutes on the road. Alex tried to shift the conversation. "I thought money was the hardest to manage."

"Nah," Lester said. "You get to be my age, health trumps everything. Money's just for making the days a little sweeter."

"What about friendships?"

"They come and they go."

"You sound a bit cynical," Alex said. "You think being in jail got to you?"

"Kid, I've been cynical my whole life. You're just noticing now because you've had a good run. You got to screw a pretty girl, and you drove all over the place independently, like a grown-up man. Things are looking up for you."

"I wish they were looking up for you too."

"At my age, all you care about are little creature comforts, like having a decent mattress, dry underwear and shoes that don't make your feet swell up like sausages."

"I like comfortable shoes." Alex crossed his right leg over his left and began caressing the new shoe.

"They're real nice," Lester said. "Take it they're from Selma."

Alex nodded and said, "I wish I would've gotten her something." He was fishing, because he assumed Lester had slipped Selma the money for the shoes. "Wonder what these things cost."

Lester snapped back. "Why can't you just appreciate a thing when you get it?"

"All right," Alex said. "Thank you."

AFTER A COUPLE of hours of driving, there was a big wedge of a sign marking their entry into South Carolina. "No going back," Lester said. "Once we pass that sign, I'm officially a fugitive. Once you take the wheel, you're officially harboring a fugitive."

"Think they'll catch us?"

"They won't know enough to look until I miss my appointment with the PO. That's a week away. I could be in goddamn Spain by then."

"Is that where you want to be?"

"Nah, I'll probably be in goddamn Schenectady, looking for a decent mattress."

"I'd like you to stay back at our house," Alex said. "I could get my mom to go along." He wasn't completely sure, but he would do his part, even if that meant reversing the deal about seeing the shrink.

"Nice of you to offer, but it's not a good idea. For one, I'd rather not live under the same roof with a woman who hates me."

"She'd learn to like you."

"I wouldn't count on that."

"Yeah, but—"

"Forget it," Lester said. "My concern is getting you home safely. And I'd like to enjoy the rest of our trip. That won't happen if you keep nagging me."

ALEX USED to believe that breaking the law was something you did only under special circumstances, when all alternative courses of action were no longer available. That was before this road trip. Now, here he was, harboring a fugitive who was sleeping in the backseat without a seatbelt on. One question settled his mind. Was he hurting anyone?

He answered no. His conscience was clear. But when he probed a little deeper, he found that his conscience was far from clear. Agreeing to kick Lester out of his house seemed sensible at the time. And it had actually worked out pretty well. They probably wouldn't have taken this trip if Lester had stayed. But now that they were returning, everything was different. Rebecca's deal with Elder Spring had expired. Lester was essentially homeless. Yet all he seemed to care about was getting Alex home safely.

"I had a dream," Lester announced groggily, still reclined on the backseat. "Not the Martin Luther King, Jr. variety. Wasn't quite that ambitious."

"What was it?" Alex asked, still wracked with guilt.

"It was you and me finding a luxury hotel, a real nice place." Lester slowly raised himself to vertical. "We played chess into the wee hours. It was a lot of fun."

"I've never played."

"That's a shame," Lester said. "And that's why I aim to teach you. There's a Hilton Hotel in Charlotte. We'll get ourselves a top-notch room."

"What about a chess board?"

"I've got a travel set in my suitcase."

Alex shook his head. "You're gonna kick my ass."

THE SUN was a hovering ball, appearing and disappearing behind gray and black skyscrapers. Alex turned the Cadillac into the valet lane at the Hilton Hotel. A man in a tux opened the driver's door and held out a ticket in exchange for car keys. Alex stepped out of the vehicle saying, "Thank you," though he wasn't exactly sure why.

"Everything's in the trunk," Lester said as he helped himself up with his stick. He stood close to Alex and whispered, "I'm paying with a credit card, but we'll need small bills. Places like this, you got to throw tip money everywhere."

Alex fished all the fives and ones out of his wallet, putting them in his front pocket for easy disbursal. They entered a marbleized lobby with lacquered wood columns. A hundred shades of color bloomed out of a crystal vase. A bellman pushed a brass cart with their luggage. It would be quite an embarrassment if they couldn't find a room after all this production.

"May I help you?" a woman with flawless skin said to Lester.

"I'd like a nice room with a view." He was struggling with his breath. "Two beds, non-smoking." He leaned his stick against the stone counter and slouched over his elbows. Alex kept a respectful distance.

The woman clicked at her computer. "We have some lovely suites still available. I can put you in one on the seventeenth floor for $209. How many nights?"

"That'll be fine, just tonight." He handed her a credit card and signed his name at the bottom of an invoice. The woman smiled a perfect-teeth-glossy-lipped smile and handed him an envelope with two key cards and free passes to the adjoining gym. The bellman held open the elevator while Lester labored his way there.

The suite was nothing like Alex's room at the Brunswick Days Inn. First thing he noticed was flowers in a vase centered on a glass-top table. Then his eyes locked onto a spectacular sunset through smoked glass. He tipped the bellman five dollars. Then he approached the window. His eyes went back and forth between the sunset and the urban landscape below.

Lester stood next to him. "This right here makes it all worthwhile."

"Is the room as nice as the one in your dream?"

"It's different, has a different feel. This one's contemporary—very chic, as they say."

"What happens next?"

"We settle in, clean up and get ourselves a nice meal at that restaurant in the lobby." He paused for breath. "Don't eat too much, or you'll really take a whuppin' come chess-time."

"Sounds good," Alex said.

"After a game or two, I'll take myself a bath—wash everything jail-related right out of me. You can go down to that gym and run to your heart's content, if you still got the energy."

The plan felt like a good match to go along with the beautiful sunset and this chic, contemporary suite.

LESTER HAD so hyped up the game of chess over dinner that the idea of actually playing felt anticlimactic for Alex. But the last thing he wanted was let the old man down. If Lester wanted to play chess, then that's exactly what they would do.

Lester pulled the set out of his suitcase and handed it to Alex. "Put it on the table and move that vase. Chess and flowers don't go together." Then he sat down and pointed to the arena where the Carolina Panthers played. "Stadium's empty, and it'll stay that way another month. What a ridiculous waste to keep all those lights on."

Alex filled two glasses of iced water and placed them on the table.

"I'll have a beer," Lester said. "And no, you can't have one...not on my watch."

It was the first time Lester had expressed an interest in drinking since they'd met. "You sure you're allowed to drink?"

"One won't do anything. Two might kill me, but I'll stick with one."

Alex wondered how many of the old man's medicine bottles warned against drinking alcohol, but he dutifully went to the mini fridge and announced there was Michelob, Heineken and Miller Lite.

"I'll take a Michelob." Lester began setting up the board, assigning himself the black pieces, Alex the white. "Here's how it goes," he said. "First, you put the board so that you got a white square to your right. *White's right*—remember that for chess, but not in real life. And always put your pieces like this." He named the chessmen: king, queen, bishop, knight, rook and pawn. He demonstrated what each of them could do.

Alex was confused but nodded anyway. Then Lester explained how the king and the rook could flip around in one fell swoop and how the lowly pawn could advance to become a queen. To further increase the confusion level, he gave the rule of *en passant*.

"It's a lot to remember," Alex said.

"Just think of this board as an ancient battlefield. We're at war. Our pride and property are at stake." He picked up both kings. "Only one of these can rule the land. How we manage our troops, offensively and defensively, dictates whose king survives." He put the pieces back and took another sip. "Let's start with a practice game."

Alex began by moving pawn, then knight, then bishop and getting each taken away in quick order. Lester demonstrated a checkmate in six moves.

"God, that was stupid," Alex said.

"Not stupid, just naïve. You're starting to learn."

In their first official game, Alex played defensively. He moved pawn after pawn after pawn, creating a W of protection from attack. Meanwhile, Lester broke through with a combination of bishop and queen. The game was over in eight moves.

"You crucified me," Alex said.

"Play like that and you deserve to be crucified." Lester downed half his beer. "Sweet taste of victory. Now let's try another game. You set up the board." He got up and made his way to the bathroom. Alex lined up the pieces as he remembered, and he rehearsed and visualized what each of them could do. He was hovering over the board when Lester returned.

"Looks like you're ready to go." The old man lowered himself into his chair. "Go on, make your move."

Alex went on the offensive. He started with one knight then the other. He moved two pawns to engage both bishops. Then he brought out his queen, only to get her taken away by Lester's black bishop.

"Gotcha," Lester said.

"I should've seen it coming," Alex said. "I suck."

"You're just too pumped up, too aggressive. You've got to see the board more clearly."

Six more moves and Lester called checkmate. "You're learning, kid. Let's try one last game."

It was true what they say about defeat being a good teacher. For nearly thirty minutes they squared off, man to man, attacking and whittling away each other's defenses. By the end of it, Alex was reduced to two pawns and a knight while Lester retained his queen, three pawns and a bishop. He called "Check" for the last time and smiled at Alex.

"You got me," Alex said.

"Yeah, but you held your own. Keep it up and you'll be a fine chess player." He drank the last of his beer and slowly got up from the table.

"Hope we can play again soon."

"Me too," Lester said. "Right now I got me a date with a whirlpool tub. I'm not passing that up."

CHAPTER TWENTY-SIX

Alex dreamt that he was living in another country—a superior country filled with smoked-glass skyscrapers, marble chessboards and tanned women in sports bras, jogging next to him, smiling glossy smiles. He awoke to the sinking realization that it was all coming to an end. By evening he'd be home again, arguing with his mother.

One way to carry on the spirit of the trip was to take home free stuff, and there was plenty. After his shower, he scurried around the place, picking up pens and stationary, a bar of soap for the body, one for the face, a little bottle of shampoo and a moisturizer. And even though he doubted he'd ever use them, he took drink coasters, a shower cap and a miniature sewing kit. It didn't matter. His aim was tangible reminders.

Then came the final luxury—room-service breakfast. Alex dragged the table to the window so that he and Lester could watch the city materialize. A man in a tux sans jacket pushed a cart to the table and unloaded two covered plates, juice and a thermal pot of coffee. Alex sent the man off with a five dollar tip.

"Ought to be good," Lester said, pouring coffee into a mug.

Alex was surprised to find that his Belgian waffle was still warm seventeen floors from its origin. "Real good," he said. He looked out the window and saw a fair amount of traffic on the interstate but only a few vehicles on the city streets and even fewer pedestrians. He asked Lester about it.

"That's because it's Sunday, and it's Charlotte. That's the problem with these modern cities—you gotta drive everywhere, makes everybody fat. And this city's one of the fattest."

"People looked pretty fit in the gym."

"That's 'cause they're tourists, and they're gym people." He spread his arms broadly. "This hotel is a palace in a Third World country. That's the fate of the American City—slums and palaces, slums and palaces."

"You sure you're not being cynical again?"

"Actually, you're the one who ought to be cynical. You'll be living in the kind of world I'm describing."

"Unless things change," Alex said.

"Spoken like a true optimist. You'll be all right, though. Maybe someday you'll get yourself a palace."

Last thing Alex wanted was a palace. What he really wanted was a way to get rid of his all-pervading guilt. Being in this tower of opulence made it worse. And it didn't help that Lester was paying for everything, asking nothing of Alex.

When they arrived at the lobby to check out, he looked away from the counter so he wouldn't have to see the final bill. He waited until Lester folded the receipt and stuffed it into his pocket.

"Thank you," Alex said timidly while patting Lester on the shoulder.

"I should thank you," Lester said. "I wouldn't have enjoyed this place by myself. You made it special."

If only you knew the real me, Alex was thinking. He pulled out the valet ticket and handed it to the attendant.

Lester was making a big deal about the fact that his energy level was good. "I could go a round or two with the champ," he said, which meant he was first to drive. When the car arrived, Alex relinquished five more dollars and slid into the passenger seat. The sky was cloudless, and it gave off a merciless heat.

In a little while, they passed Statesville, which made him recall his rain-soaked driving lesson and how he had almost smacked into a pickup truck, but instead earned the right to drive on this very highway. Why couldn't he feel like that now?

"You been quiet awhile," Lester said. "What's bugging you?"

"It's nothing," Alex said.

"I don't even have to look at you to know that's a lie. Go ahead, cough it up."

But Alex just sat there, wondering what he could say to evade the truth. He could reveal smaller truths, like how he was dreading that first conversation with his mother. Or how concerned he was about Lester finding a place to live. But he knew those things would come out hollow, and he'd be left with the same feeling.

So he pushed aside his fear and began speaking. "It was a couple of weeks ago, right after my birthday."

"I remember it well."

"My mom got pretty upset."

"I regret saying those things. Didn't know how thin-skinned she'd be."

"She pretty much wanted you gone after that," Alex said. "And she used me to get rid of you. So on the way back from seeing my psychiatrist, she made me a deal. She said if I agreed to kicking you out, I wouldn't have to see the shrink anymore."

They passed the state line into Virginia. Lester didn't speak.

"I took the deal." Alex's voice trembled. "It was a terrible thing. And I've been sorry about it ever since." He stopped talking and braced himself for Lester's response.

"I'm not a fan of psychiatrists," Lester said. "They pretty much murdered my sister Mary, turned her into a drooling vegetable with their drugs and their electric jolts to the head."

"Right," Alex said, "but I could've handled the guy. I was flushing his drugs down the toilet."

"Goddamn drug-peddlers!" Lester clenched his hand into a gnarled fist.

"I know. But I'm the one who sold you out. I should've handled the shrink myself."

"Don't fool yourself, kid. Your mother would've found another way to get rid of me." He gave Alex a quizzical stare. "What the hell you seeing a psychiatrist for anyway?"

"He said I've got depression and behavior problems…and a poor attention span."

"You're a goddamn teenager. He ought to know better."

"So you're not angry I sold you out?"

"I'm angry, but it ain't for that reason. I'm angry at that imbecile tagging you with labels and forcing drugs on you, making you think you got some mental disease. He's a demonic fortune-teller and worse, 'cause he's got a medical license to wreak his havoc. That's what I'm angry about."

Alex nodded. He was relieved of some of the guilt but still concerned about Lester's living situation.

"And your mother," Lester continued. "I'm angry at her for putting you in a situation like that. She's nearly as bad as the shrink."

"I didn't know you as well back then. If I knew you like I do now, I wouldn't have taken the deal. Swear to God."

"I believe you, kid. It's a hell of a thing to put you through."

And that was true. What kind of a mother does a thing like that? Alex was back to his old stomping grounds—maternal anger, which also helped ease the guilt. After a period of silence, Lester said, "Forget the shrink. Forget your mother. You ought to do something for yourself."

"What's that?"

"Say that you'll never give up on yourself. That's all you've got to say. And you gotta mean it."

Alex felt a little silly. But he pushed himself to say the words with a straight face. "Okay." He cleared his throat. "I'll never give up on myself."

Lester nodded. "That's good, kid. That's your promise. Don't you forget it."

CHAPTER TWENTY-SEVEN

They wouldn't be discussing the Virginia Tech massacre on their return trip, because Lester had fallen asleep before the exit signs. So Alex was left to ponder the events of April 16, 2007 on his own. And they wouldn't be discussing all the Civil War battlefields scattered along their route, because the old man remained on the backseat sleeping his way through the entire state of Virginia. If he hadn't already proven himself a marathon napper, Alex would've been alarmed. Lester continued his slumber through those little slices of West Virginia and Maryland. He was going on five hours when they crossed the state line into Pennsylvania. Alex kept driving, but his worry was growing.

Partly out of concern and partly out of boredom, he reached back and applied a couple of nudges to wake the old man up. And it worked. As they passed Carlisle, Lester slowly rose and looked around. He coughed a couple of times and said, "We're in Pennsylvania already?"

"That's right. You missed a lot."

"I need a bathroom, but wait till we get past Harrisburg. There's never a place to piss downtown." He was fiddling with his left arm.

"Something wrong?" Alex asked.

"Arm's probably numb from sleeping on it."

They turned toward a multi-purpose gas station off the Grantville exit. Alex pulled up to a row of pumps and began filling the tank while the old man made his way to the bathroom. Fortunately, the back of his pants looked dry.

Lester was still in one of the bathroom stalls while Alex stood at a urinal, and the old man remained in the building while Alex worked a squeegee, struggling to rid the windshield of hundreds of miles of bug carnage. Finally, Lester arrived carrying a shopping bag. He opened the passenger door and said, "Looks real good. You'd need a razor blade to get'em all. Let's move."

Back on the road, they entered what Lester called the heart of Pennsylvania coal-mining country. "It's got to be about the worst job there is," he said.

"Why's that?"

"Chipping away at solid earth all day is bad enough. But you gotta do it underground, and you gotta breathe that foul air. Can't imagine anything worse." He reached into his bag and pulled out a bottle of Advil and a bottle of water.

"I guess it's not a job I'd want," Alex said.

"You find a career that engages your brain. Pay is usually better. And as long as you don't blow it with drugs, your brain'll stay sharp a lot longer than your body." He was struggling with the Advil bottle but finally got it open. "I'm all the proof you need of that." He shook four tablets onto his palm and downed them with water.

"You got a headache?"

"That I do," Lester said, and he closed his eyes.

"You're not gonna sleep again, are you?"

"Please," Lester said, "a little quiet for now."

Alex shook his head. Getting old really did suck.

Then a terrible thing happened. Lester's upper body jerked forward a couple of times while his left arm just dangled along like a dead eel. He appeared to be on the verge of vomiting, but nothing came out of him, thank God. Still, Alex grabbed the plastic shopping bag and said, "Here, take this, just in case." Last thing Lester wanted was vomit all over his interior.

But the old man didn't take it. "No," he said. Then he started to cry.

"What's wrong?"

Lester didn't respond. His eyes were closed.

"Say something!"

Lester made a series of garbled sounds. The only decipherable word was *promise*—the rest slurred beyond recognition.

Alex cut across a lane of traffic and slowed onto the shoulder, rumbling to a stop. He reached for Lester's chest. "Wake up," he said. "You'll be okay. Just wake up." He gave a shove causing Lester's head to bob forward. "No! You gotta wake up!"

If ever he needed a cell phone, now was the time. He got out of the car, faced oncoming traffic and flapped his arms for help. A white pickup truck pulled in front of the Cadillac. Alex ran to the driver's side. "Call 911!" he yelled. "Call 911!"

A man stepped out and handed Alex his phone.

"What's the address of your emergency?" asked a female dispatcher.

Somehow Alex found the capacity to explain the situation. The woman asked whether Lester had a history of stroke, heart attack or seizures.

"I don't know," Alex said three times.

"What are his medications?"

"I don't know, but I can find out."

"Good, I'm sending an ambulance right now. I'll relay the info."

Holding the phone in one hand, Alex rifled through Lester's suitcase and found the black leather bag. He started reading off the names from each bottle—long crazy names, but the woman kept saying, "Got it," so he figured he was doing okay.

He could hear a siren gaining in volume. He thanked her and returned the phone to the pickup driver. "Hope your friend makes it," the man said as he got back into his truck.

"Me too," Alex said, and that's when he began to cry.

Two paramedics got out of the ambulance and proceeded to hoist Lester's limp body onto a gurney.

"Please be okay," Alex said as he returned to the Cadillac. The ambulance sped away, siren howling. Alex took off behind them.

It didn't matter how fast the ambulance was going or if a trooper was on his ass, he refused to give ground. They got off the interstate at Frackville and raced through one red light after another. The Cadillac chirped and bounced and swayed through turns. It could have gone faster, which made him worry even more about Lester's prognosis.

A shiny black sign read Anthracite Regional Medical Center, and the four-story structure loomed a quarter mile up a hill. There was a roundabout with three options, one of which was the emergency entrance. Alex separated from the ambulance. The first open parking spot had a sign, Reserved for Dr. Calvin Sprague. Alex didn't give a shit about Dr. Sprague. He shot right in and ran for the emergency doors.

All the action ran up and down a hall leading to double doors, but you couldn't pass the doors without being nabbed by the woman at the reception desk. He approached and said, "My friend's in there. I gotta see him."

"What's his name?" she asked, her voice weighed down by boredom.

"Lester Bray. He just came in."

She nodded. "He's next in line for a CT scan. You'll have to wait out here." She gestured to a roomful of chairs. "I'll let you know when he's out."

Alex went over to the waiting area, which featured a stone waterfall, of all things. He sat next to it and tried looking at a magazine about celebrities, but he couldn't get past his own thoughts. He put the magazine down and stared into the bubbling pool of water and the dozens of coins that lay below. Each coin, he figured, was tossed in the hope of a favorable medical outcome. Later, a janitor would come along and scoop out the change for cigarette money. That's how the universe balanced itself out. Even so, Alex found himself reaching into his pocket for a quarter. He clutched it between both palms and said a little prayer. "Please, God, make Lester well again." Then he plopped it into the water. He leaned back and closed his eyes.

When he had first sat down, he thought of how silly it was to have a waterfall in a hospital. He imagined some flimsy spiritual advisor at the hospital groundbreaking pleading his case to the architect. But somehow the continuous rippling and gurgling had a positive effect. When the monotone receptionist finally called his name, Alex sprang to his feet with a renewed sense of hope.

"He's been transferred to Neurology, Room 316." She pointed to a set of elevators.

WHATEVER HOPE he had garnered by the waterfall was dashed when he entered Room 316. A nurse with rhinoceros hips hovered over Lester's unconscious body. She was attaching electrodes to his chest while checking an amber screen. Someone had already hooked up oxygen to his nose and poked a line into his left arm, leading up to a bag of clear fluid. There was an empty bag with a thicker hose hanging from the bed-frame. The business end of that hose was probably connected to Lester's penis. Thankfully, the old man's body was under sheets.

The nurse rotated away from the machine. "You here to see Mr. Bray?"

"Yeah," Alex said, "how is he?"

"He's in a coma, I'm sorry to report."

Lester's eyes were closed and his face sagged, especially on the right side. A bloodstained bandage stretched across his right temple. Dried blood freckled the upper portion of his right ear. His bed was positioned at a slight incline, which would have been ideal for viewing the TV mounted on the opposite wall. But, like the off-television, there didn't seem to be much going on in Lester's head. Aside from breathing, there was nothing. Not even a vacant stare.

Alex was near tears again. To fend them off, he needed some form of action. "Anything I can do?" he asked.

"You can sit and talk to him," she said. "Hold his hand if you want. You never know if something's getting in."

Alex dragged a chair next to the bed. The nurse went around and patted Alex's back, which seemed to intensify his sadness, like she was prodding it out of him. He tried to keep his feelings inside, but he wasn't strong enough.

She continued patting while he went on crying. After a little while, she said, "Wish I could stay longer, but I've got other patients. You stay here as long as you like. Press the call button if you need anything." Before leaving the room, she adjusted Lester's sheet even though it didn't need adjusting.

LESTER'S RIGHT hand was directly in front of Alex. He touched it and said, "Hey Lester, you're scaring me. You've gotta get well again. We've got more driving to do, more places to see."

To the knobby hand, he added, "I was thinking maybe I could be your permanent chauffeur. That's what I was thinking. I wouldn't ask for anything—no money or anything. I'd just drive you around wherever you want to go."

He went on to recount some of the finer moments of their trip so far. "Breakfast at the Fort Lauderdale pier, Ernie's Catfish Shack and chess at the Hilton—those are my top three. Well, except for Selma, of course."

He talked about drawing and driving and his newly discovered joy of running. "I hated running before this trip," he said. "I don't know what happened. It just feels different now. The shoes help." When he ran out of things to say, he went over to the nurses' station and found a separated copy of the *Reading Eagle*. He read out loud, cherry-picking articles from every section, minus the obituaries. "Yankees took a doubleheader against the Devil Rays," he said and read the story with all its mind-numbing numerical detail. "This one looks interesting. A New Jersey woman paddled a canoe from Miami to Maine." He read about the woman's adventures, which actually seemed tame compared to his own travels.

"Here's one you'll love. For two and a half hours, Dick Cheney served as acting president while Bush was under sedation for a medical procedure. Feel free to insert your own joke." He glanced over at Lester's droopy face. No joke there.

Alex kept reading and watching for movement. He was looking for a slight twitch, which could occur at any moment. That's what he was waiting for. Just a flinch. Then everything else would gradually return.

AS DARKNESS spread across the world outside the hospital window, it occurred to Alex that he should call his mother. She was probably worried and definitely pissed. But after what he'd been through, he could handle whatever she threw at him.

He picked up the phone next to Lester's bed and got an outside line. The recorded voice informed him that the hospital charged three dollars a minute for long distance calls. Worth it? Probably not, but he dialed his mother's cell anyway.

"Hello?" she said.

"Hey, mom, it's me."

"Alex! My God! Where are you?"

"I'm in a hospital with Lester. He's in a coma." He felt himself turning to tears again, but he wasn't going to cry in front of his mother, not even over the phone.

"I'm very sorry to hear that, Alex."

"Sure you are," he said.

"I am, really, but I suspected something like this might happen."

"It's only a coma. He'll come out of it. He'll be fine."

"I'll say a prayer for him," she said. "Meanwhile, I'm coming down there. Last time I checked, you were sixteen years old. That means I'm still in charge."

"You don't even know where I am," he said but suspected that he'd already blown it.

"I've got the number, Alex. Wherever you are, I'm on my way."

"You can come," Alex said, now focusing acutely on Lester's hand. "But I'm not leaving without him...not until he's well again." This would have been the perfect time for the hand to flinch, for Lester's eyes to open, for his mouth to say the words, "Where am I, kid?" It would have been the perfect thing.

"I'll be there soon," his mother said. "I love you."

That certainly wasn't what he wanted to hear. He hung up the phone. And he started crying again.

In a little while, the same wide-hipped nurse showed up carrying a tray with covered food and two drinks. She set it down on a rolling table and wheeled it close. Alex glanced at Lester's face and said, "He won't be able to eat that."

She nodded. "It's for you. I got it from the kitchen before they closed." She lifted the plastic cover. "I won't vouch for the quality."

"Thanks," he said. Hunger hadn't crossed his mind until the smell of food was brought before him. He guessed the meat was turkey. There was a scoop of mashed potatoes next to a pile of green beans, all cut the same length.

She pointed and said, "That chair you're sitting in folds out to make a bed. It's not comfortable, but it's better than sleeping on the floor." She stepped back and maneuvered herself toward a cabinet. She pulled out a pillow, a sheet and a blue blanket and placed each of these on Lester's bed, taking care not to impinge the old man's feet.

"Thanks again," Alex said. "You really don't mind if I sleep here?"

"We do what we can for out-of-towners. Normally that means

extended visiting hours." She smiled down on him. "We're pushing it a little further for you."

He was grateful and terrified at the same time. He didn't mind being a charity case. In fact, his whole life seemed to be about accepting others' charities. But why was she being so nice? Was it because of his youth, or was she doing it out of the hopelessness of Lester's condition?

He didn't dare ask.

CHAPTER TWENTY-EIGHT

Of all the places he had slept over the past ten days, this was by far the worst. The opened chair was like sleeping on railroad timbers, and the blanket wasn't thick enough to fend off the air-conditioned chill. But he could tolerate these inconveniences. What horrified him was the uneven quality of Lester's breathing. It seemed to catch, stop altogether, sputter and then somehow gasp back into rhythm. Over the course of the night, Alex had pressed the red button three times, and on each occasion some unimpressed nurse came in and told him not to worry.

By four o'clock, he was done pretending sleep would come. He got up, reconfigured the sinister chair and jogged down to the Cadillac to retrieve his drawing materials. He wanted to attempt a picture of Lester. This had become his sleep-deprived mission. But when he returned, he couldn't bear to focus on the face before him. It wasn't the bandage or the tube crossing under the old man's nose that bothered him. It was the whole face. It was the feeling that if he drew that face, as opposed to the one he knew, he'd be violating their friendship.

But Lester's hand was a different story. It hadn't changed since the day they met—same arthritic bulges, same wrinkles and splotches. You could say there was something grotesque about it, hardly even hand-like at all. In fact, it looked more like a gnarly tree, way past its prime but still holding to life. "That's it!" Alex said out loud. That's what he would draw. He turned the chair to capture Lester's hand from the best angle, and he opened his sketchbook.

From boney wrist and the valleys between metacarpals, the drawing started as the unmistakable form of Lester's right hand. But where fingers terminated, branches began. And these gave rise to new branches. New hands. His mind was soaring. He got out a piece of charcoal and shaded the areas obscured from the sun by veins, by knots.

He stepped back to evaluate his work. From a distance, he had sketched an ancient maple in the stillness of winter. But up close, it was all interconnected hands, reaching out in every direction. As he finished shading the last portion, the sun had risen to the level of the hospital room window. As a final step, to lock the drawing in time, he pulled out his can of fixative spray.

He gave one last satisfied appraisal, and then he looked over at Lester's face. It was the same lifeless face with the blood-stained bandage and the oxygen tube. But if Alex didn't know any better—and he wasn't exactly sure—he would've sworn the old man's mouth was ever-so-slightly grinning.

A BREAKFAST tray arrived, which made him sad all over again, because it had Lester's name on it next to the word *diabetic*. Lester should have been the one eating it. Instead, his nutrients came by way of a bag, one drip-drop at a time.

As Alex ate the last of the scrambled eggs, he heard a light knock on the open door. He looked up. There stood Rebecca dressed in blue jeans and a blouse the color of coffee with cream. He didn't know whether he ought to be aroused or angry. Next to Rebecca stood his mother.

Rebecca was first to speak. "Hi Alex," she said. Her eyes were red and wet. "It's such an awful thing." She went right over to Lester.

"Glad you're okay," his mother said. She tried to reach for Alex's arm. "Looks like you've been taking care of yourself."

"You can't make me ditch him this time," Alex said. "You can't bribe me."

"I wouldn't do that." She pulled a tissue out of her purse, even though her eyes were as dry as little moons.

There were so many ways he could hurt her without even raising a finger. And, given what she had done with his father's letters and her deal to get rid of Lester, it was irresistible. He looked straight at her and said, "Lester's coma is your fault."

She jolted back a step. "That's ridiculous, Alex, and you know it!"

"I know a lot. Being away from you has brightened my horizons."

Rebecca spoke up. "Don't you mean *broadened* your horizons?"

"Yeah, that too."

"Well, I'm glad you've had your little enlightenment," his mother said. "Isn't it convenient for you to blame the one person who's cared for you all these years?" She thrust her tissue in front of him. "But I know why you do it. You do it because you know I'll always stand by you."

"Okay you two," Rebecca said. "Let's get a little perspective here. This is about Mr. Bray, bless his soul. I pray to God he gets well again. And I confess I've got a hand in all of this." She shook her head. "If there's blame to go around, I deserve some of it."

"No you don't," Alex said. "You didn't do anything wrong." He pointed to his mother. "There's no need to protect her."

"All I'm saying is that it was my idea to put y'all together. I was so excited about the prospects. I thought you'd make such a good match."

"Perhaps your eagerness did get a little ahead of you," his mother said.

"No, Rebecca," Alex said. "Don't listen to her. What you did was the best thing. It was the best thing ever."

And that's when it started. Of all the times and places to cry, this was the worst. He snatched the dry tissue out of his mother's hand and retreated to the window.

A LITTLE MAN with a white lab coat entered the room and announced he was Lester's neurologist. The man couldn't have been taller than five feet in heels, and he couldn't have weighed more than a hundred pounds after a Chinese buffet. He looked up at Rebecca and spoke to her as if she was Lester's closest kin. In a way, she was, because she had been designated as the old man's health care proxy. The doctor asked if he could speak openly in front of Alex and his mother.

Rebecca looked at each and said, "That would be fine."

The doctor began speaking, "Mr. Bray had a subarachnoid hemorrhage with substantial bleeding. It's basically a ruptured aneurism. To reduce the pressure, we performed a craniotomy. And there was quite a lot of blood." Alex caught the doctor's eyes glancing at the contour of Rebecca's fine breasts. At least the man had good taste. "And I'm afraid there's been damage," he continued. "We won't know the extent until we do another scan, and that won't be necessary if he stays in a coma."

Alex found nothing positive in these words. He tuned out the rest of the monologue and squinted at the doctor's name badge. Last name started with B, which ruled out Dr. Sprague. At least Alex hadn't stolen the little man's parking spot.

THE DAY consisted of sitting at Lester's bedside, talking and reading out loud and staring at the same withered hand, hoping for signs of life. Even though Alex wasn't opposed to the hospital food, his mother and Rebecca brought him a roast beef sandwich for lunch and a twelve-inch pepperoni pizza for dinner. It was during dinner that Rebecca announced she was leaving. "You've got my number if anything changes," she told his mother. Then she reached for Alex's hand. "I'll be thinking of you and praying for Mr. Bray."

"Thanks," Alex said. He wanted to give her a hug. But he knew that would start him crying all over again.

His mother had made motel reservations, and she insisted that he stay with her. The last thing he wanted was to sleep in the same room with her, and he didn't want to abandon Lester, even for one night. But the prospect of an actual mattress and no medical interruptions won him over. He got into her car and kept his eyes closed all the way through Frackville. He could have slept for days. That's how he felt.

But after just a few hours, he startled himself awake. He looked at the motel clock—3:48. His mind returned to Lester's words before they were pulled over by the trooper. *All my family members died alone.* That's what he had said. It was the family curse, and it would happen to him. Lester was alone right now.

Alex sat up and looked around the motel room. His mother was motionless in the other queen bed, her head and body oriented to the far wall. Her keys lay on the nightstand between the two beds. Just looking at them wrong could make them jingle.

He put on the same shirt from the previous day, and then he knelt down in front of the nightstand, inching the keys forward, keeping their chiseled ends separated from each other. When they got to the edge, he pinched and pulled them up. The hum of the air-conditioner was his greatest ally. He glanced once again at the back of his mother's head before closing the door. Maybe she was right about what she had said. In her own way, maybe she really had always stood by him. Even when that meant hurting another person.

The Lexus had a tight feel, gripping the road like super glue compared to the Cadillac's silly putty. But Alex missed the old Caddy. It was gratifying to see that it was still there in Dr. Sprague's spot. Next spot over was reserved for a Dr. Michael Fallon—no B. Lester's miniature neurologist was spared again.

Alex didn't bother with the elevator. He ran up the stairs to Lester's floor and almost ran past Room 316. The door was closed. That was odd.

"Can I help you?" It was a man's voice.

Alex was winded. He turned and recognized the man as one of the attendants from the previous night. "Yeah, I'm here to see Lester. This is his room."

"Not anymore," the attendant said. "I'm really sorry, but Mr. Bray expired about an hour ago. He's been taken to the morgue."

The words *expired* and *morgue* smashed against the insides of Alex's head. He couldn't imagine words like that being spoken to him. "There's no way," he said.

"I'm really sorry for your loss."

Alex dropped to the floor and snapped his head against the plastic handrail. "No way," he said, "no fucking way!"

HE JUST sat there for a while, angry with himself, angry at the world, missing Lester. Nobody bothered him while he sat and cried, not caring to wipe his eyes. He tried to appreciate the totality of Lester's death and the loss it signified, but his thoughts kept going to the morgue, as if it held some dark magnetism.

Alex hardly knew what he was doing when he rose from the floor and went over to the nurse's station. The same attendant was writing in a chart. A petite nurse with burgundy hair sat nearby. He remembered her from the previous night when he'd pressed the call button. She was all business, but not in a rude way. And she liked to chew gum. Behind the counter she was chomping away while peeling labels and placing them on urine sample cups. "I want to see him," Alex said.

The nurse stopped chewing and looked at him. Then she peered over at the attendant, who gave a nod. She got up and said, "I'll take you myself."

Alex struggled against his tears as he entered the elevator with the nurse, and he said nothing all the way down to the basement level. The only sound was the gum-smacking nurse. The door opened, and he followed her down a hall. She stopped and pressed a button. A bearded man in aqua scrubs opened the door.

"Closest kin needs to identify Lester Bray," the nurse said.

The man gave a double-take as he appraised Alex, but then said, "Fine with me."

The room was cold—not exactly a meat locker but close. A sheet-covered body lay on a gurney. It had to be Lester, because it was the only horizontal body around. It was silly to be afraid of a dead man, Alex told himself, but the fear remained. The bearded man didn't give Alex time to adjust. He went right over and flipped the sheet down to expose Lester's head and torso.

Alex felt a surge of fear as he got closer and stood next to Lester's shut-eyed face. The bandage was gone, and there weren't any tubes connected to bags, no gowns and no beeping machines. If there was anything good about coming down here, that was it. Lester wasn't a patient anymore.

The nurse was kind enough to stop chewing her gum, making the room totally silent. Alex placed a hand on Lester's chest and tried to remain perfectly still. He was keenly aware of the breath coming in and out of him and the lack of breath coming from Lester. And that's when it hit him.

Lester's final words in the Cadillac. The only clear word was *promise*, but there was more. Even as Lester had struggled with a brain-bursting headache; even as he fought off an urge to vomit; even as his left arm succumbed to paralysis; even as he cried, knowing that death was near, he didn't think of himself. He thought of Alex.

Last thing Lester had said was, "Don't forget your promise."

Alex broke down crying again. He looked at Lester's face and whispered, "I won't. I'll never give up on myself."

CHAPTER TWENTY-NINE

Right smack in the middle, between Lester's death and funeral, Alex had an appointment with the shrink. In the spirit of reasserting her role as power broker, his mother had arranged the session. But, ironically, he was perfectly willing to go.

He had stayed up most of the night working on two speeches—one for Lester's funeral, the other for Dr. Kruger. On the ride over in his mother's Lexus, Alex didn't wear his baseball cap, and he didn't try to distract himself with *New Yorker* cartoons in the waiting room. He merely sat there, mentally rehearsing what he would say.

"Come on back, Alex," Dr. Kruger said. Then he looked at his mother and said, "Patricia, give us five minutes before joining us." It was an unexpected move on the doctor's part. Alex would have to adjust accordingly.

"So, Alex," Dr. Kruger said as he closed the office door, "I won't pretend not to know what's been going on over the past two weeks. Your mother and I had a few conversations."

"I'm sure you got an unbiased account." Alex sat down.

"I'm not here to reprimand you. In fact, I think I can understand the motives for what you did."

"What did I do?"

Dr. Kruger chuckled and said, "Where do I start?" He leaned forward. "You ran off without telling anyone—"

"Not true," Alex interrupted. "I wrote a note."

"Okay," Dr. Kruger said. "But then you took off from Florida instead of going with your mother."

"Well, that part is true. But I don't regret anything. I'd do it exactly the same again."

"So you don't mind putting your mother through hell?"

"She's fine," Alex said. "She and Bill had a nice little vacation on the beach. She even got herself a much-needed tan."

"She wasn't fine when she called my home after midnight. Twice."

"So maybe you need a vacation."

Dr. Kruger shook his head and took a long breath.

"I'm not going to apologize to her, if that's what you want. And I won't apologize to you for missing a little beauty rest."

Dr. Kruger actually laughed at that. "None needed," he said. "Shall we hear what your mother has to say?"

"Not yet." Alex reached into his back pocket and pulled out a couple of folded pages. "There's something I need to bring up with you."

"Sure," Dr. Kruger said, "anything at all."

"Last time I was here, you practically called me a murderer."

"I was expressing a degree of concern."

"Well, that's good, because I'm here to do the same for you."
Alex unfolded the pages and placed them on the doctor's desk.
The headline read: *Massachusetts girl's fatal overdose raises questions
about psychiatric drugs for children*. Alex had gotten the article off the
internet. It was four months old—not as timely as the newsprint

Kruger had shown him. But it would serve the purpose.

"I'm aware of this case," Dr. Kruger said, reclining away from his desk.

"The girl was four years old," Alex said. "Four years old and diagnosed with ADHD and Bipolar Disorder. She was forced to take drugs by one of your shrink colleagues. When those didn't do the job, she got more drugs and higher doses." This might have been the longest thing Alex had ever said to the man, but it felt good. Really good. He kept going. "The girl's preschool nurse described her as a 'floppy doll' before she dropped dead from overdose."

Dr. Kruger nodded and said, "You raise a good point. This may indeed turn out to be a case of malpractice." He was still reclined and looking casual, but his fidgeting right leg gave him away. "For my part," Kruger continued, "I don't medicate four year olds."

"Nice defense," Alex said. "And I don't shoot my classmates. I don't own a gun. I don't know how to make a bomb, and I suck at violent video games. Between you and me, who do you think is more likely to end up a murderer?"

Dr. Kruger didn't answer. And he didn't need to, because someone saved him by knocking on the door. He sat up a bit straighter and said, "Come in."

The receptionist opened the door. "I have Patricia Riley."

"Fine, have her come in." Dr. Kruger refolded the article and tucked it under the medical chart. "We can revisit this," he said, almost whispering to Alex.

"I'm sure you'd like that."

Alex's mother came into the office and sat in the chair next to Alex, placing her purse on her lap.

"We were just having a very productive conversation," Alex said to his mother.

She looked at the doctor and said, "Is that so?"

"In a way, yes," Dr. Kruger said. "We were talking about medication."

"So you told Alex what I found?"

"Not exactly. It was more a discussion about the dangers of overmedication."

"Well, I don't see the relevance of that." Alex's mother looked from the doctor to Alex, "Especially in light of what I found."

"Perhaps you could tell him," Dr. Kruger said.

Alex was starting to worry. This had the makings of a two-on-one fight.

"All right," Patricia said, still looking at Alex. "You haven't been taking your medications, at least not since your absence. You left all three bottles in your bathroom."

Shit, Alex thought. Stupidest oversight imaginable. He had been so caught up with packing the things he actually needed that he hadn't even thought about the meds.

"Tell me," Dr. Kruger said. "And don't lie. When was the last time you actually took your prescribed medications?"

"Why does it even matter?" Alex said. "I don't need them. I stopped taking them a long time ago. I'm fine without them."

Kruger raised his clasped hands to his mouth as if to remind himself to think before speaking. Alex's mother cut right through the silence. "Anybody who does what you did is not fine."

"What about you?" Alex said. "Mail theft is a federal crime! And you've been doing it for years. All I did was visit my father, because you wouldn't take me."

"You did far more than that!"

"Let's cool down for a moment," Dr. Kruger said. And it appeared as though the shrink had already taken his own advice. He actually seemed calm for a man whose patient was totally noncompliant and whose same patient nearly called him a child killer. "I think I can understand Alex's perspective here," he continued. "And I think this may be an appropriate time for a change. Considering Alex's good grades and the positive friendship he recently shared, I propose something new. I'm going to discontinue all current prescriptions."

"Wow," Alex said in disbelief. He sat up a bit straighter, suddenly wishing he would've called the man a murderer long before now. He looked at Kruger and said, "You won't regret it."

The shrink returned eye contact. "I trust not," he said, which seemed to cover more territory than the immediate situation.

"Wait a minute," Alex's mother said. "That's it? After everything I've told you, that's all you have to say?"

"I guess there is more, Patricia." Dr. Kruger hesitated, and then he said, "I'd like you to stop taking your son's mail."

CHAPTER THIRTY

Lester's funeral was held four days after his death on a cloudy Saturday in Schenectady, New York. Alex had insisted on driving the Cadillac, and he insisted on keeping Lester's stick behind the front seat instead of the trunk, which was where his mother had wanted to put it. She sat in the backseat, prodding it away from her as if the thing was someone else's used handkerchief. Rebecca sat up front, instructing Alex where to make his turns.

The funeral home was across the street from a park with tennis courts. The building looked like a Dutch mansion. "Looks haunted," Alex said as he searched for a parking spot.

Rebecca smiled. "It's the nicest funeral home in Schenectady. Mr. Bray had a lot of class."

One thing Alex hadn't yet learned was how to parallel park, and he wasn't about to try it now with Rebecca in the car. He drove on to the next block and found an easy spot. He looked back at his mother and said, "Hand me the stick, please."

She brought it forward. "I hope you're not planning on putting this in his casket."

"Yup," he said, "I am."

"You can't do that."

"It's his stick, and that's where he wanted me to put it." Alex began walking and poking his way along the sidewalk. A big tuxedoed man held open the door for everyone. Last time Alex received such courtesy was at the Hilton in Charlotte. He let his mother and Rebecca pass before him.

The room was filled with approximately equal parts black and white people—all wearing suits or dresses. Alex wore khakis and a short-sleeve red shirt. It was the same combo he'd worn on the day he picked up Lester from jail and sat across from him at the truck stop in Brunswick. He had chosen the attire out of nostalgia, not realizing that he would stand out like a pimp at a Lutheran church. It made him feel nervous and judged.

With the exception of his mother and Rebecca, he didn't expect to know anybody. It would have been great if Selma and Earlene had made the trip, but Rebecca said they couldn't. He nodded pleasantly at a few people while stepping his way around the crowd. His goal was to get into the chapel before everyone else and put the stick in Lester's casket. If the old man's fingers were clutched around it, no one would have the nerve to pull it out.

The casket was glossy black with brass inlay near the edges, and it was surrounded on three sides by a cascade of flower bouquets. As he came closer, he could see the flared tip of Lester's nose. The same anxiety from the morgue returned. He couldn't imagine seeing dead people on a regular basis. Lester's face was made up nicely with some kind of powder or paste, and his expression looked peaceful, like he was simply indulging in one of his marathon naps. It didn't fit that he was dressed in a fancy suit, but at least it was respectable. The stick would make it even better. Alex glanced back at the front of the room. Everyone was still out in the lounge.

His innards clenched as he reached for the old man's hand. It was cold and stiff, and it gave him a terrible chill. It didn't seem at all like the hand he had sketched five days earlier. If he tried to bend the fingers, he'd risk snapping them off. The easiest thing was to lay the stick under the old man's forearm.

So that's what he did. He took one final look then drifted back to the first pew. He tried to picture Lester in the afterlife, possessing all the things lacking in his prior existence—vibrant health, a loving wife and even a couple of kids. In a little while, a line formed in front of the casket. Alex closed his eyes. A woman played something slow and depressing on a portable organ while a string of people passed before him.

The music picked up a bit and then stopped altogether. Everyone was seated except for an old black man with chaotic white hair. He let a moment pass. Then he said, "Today we celebrate and honor the life of Lester Bray." He opened his hand toward the casket. "Here was a man who grew up with nothing. He came from a poor town in Alabama. He struggled to make a place for himself in this world. And let me tell you, folks, he found a place."

Alex was too nervous to continue listening. And he wouldn't allow himself to cry. He had already honored Lester with an abundance of tears. Today he would honor the old man with words from the heart, spoken publicly. He had written his speech on Hilton stationary. Putting his thoughts to paper was the easy part. The prospect of actually reading it out loud in front of all these people put him on the verge of terror.

Three more people got up to speak on Lester's behalf. One man, a former co-worker, recounted the glory days at GE and how valuable Lester still was to the diesel locomotive industry. An elderly woman spoke of being neighborly as one of the finest virtues of mankind and how helpful Lester was as her neighbor. Then a middle-aged white man, a lawyer, declared Lester a beacon of community service. He recounted how Lester had pestered the mayor into condemning a row of crack houses and allocating more funds for the downtown library expansion.

Alex's nerves were a nonstop crescendo. The fact that these other people expressed themselves so eloquently made it even worse. He craved for at least one of them to screw up, take the pressure off. This would have been an ideal time for the Father Mind Game. Alex could have gotten a major lift knowing that his father was there in spirit, guiding him to oratory perfection. But the game had spoiled into something childish and stupid. The wild-haired man regained the pulpit and said, "Is there anyone else who would like to share in Lester's memory?"

A spell of silence. The moment had come. Alex was approaching spontaneous combustion, but he cleared his throat and said, "I'll say something."

"Come on up," the man said.

He stood, pulled his speech from his back pocket and took a wavering route to the podium. The man gave him a gentle pat on the back and said, "Say what's in your heart," which didn't help, because Alex's heart was choked off by all the anxiety. He was alone, staring at a kaleidoscope of people.

"Hello," he said, "my name is Alex Riley." Just then he remembered a technique an English teacher had given his class. She had insisted that you should always direct your voice to a person in the back row. So he picked an oval-faced black woman who was standing near the door. She was wearing a fancy hat and a royal blue dress that shimmered when she changed position. And as she waited for Alex to speak, she changed position a lot.

"It's okay, honey." It was a different woman, third row center. "Just say what's on your mind." Suddenly it occurred to him that he could play the game one last time. Just the thought of it helped him relax.

He brought the calm wisdom of his father to the center of his mind and started reading the speech. "Friendship isn't measured by the amount of time you spend together. It isn't measured by how many things you have in common, like sports teams or political parties. True friendship, I've recently discovered, goes a lot deeper."

The woman from the third row said, "That's right."

"I know this because of the brief time I spent with Lester, traveling around the country. What I found is that friendship can happen between an old black man and a scrawny white punk like me."

An eruption of laughter filled the room, and it seemed to warm the chilly cavity of Alex's chest. He continued reading: "And I discovered that the best thing about Lester's friendship was that he didn't judge me." As he said this, he realized it wasn't totally accurate. "Well," he continued, disregarding his notes, "not unless I needed it. And he didn't pin labels on me. But he did listen to me for hours and hours. And I listened to him the best I could."

He paused and glanced down at his notes. He had written down some of the highlights of their trip, but he didn't feel like covering all that. He decided to go a different direction. Looking at the iridescent woman, he said, "Lester wasn't afraid to break the rules. In fact, he and

I were never supposed to travel together—he wasn't even supposed to drive. Lester took naps in the backseat without his seatbelt on, and he stole a couple of hand towels out of a motel room to keep his car from getting dirty. So he wasn't perfect." There was some chuckling from the audience. "That's probably why I liked him so much." More chuckles.

"Then there was the day he whacked a racist cop with his walking stick. He did it to protect me—*me* of all people. I didn't even have a friend before Lester. And this old man protected me. He showed me what it means to have a true friend." Alex glanced over at the casket. "By the way, his stick is there now. He wanted it with him."

He looked back at the audience. "But friendship is also a two-way street. And I was lucky enough to be able to do something good for Lester. With some help—some pretty big help—I was able to spring him from jail. That's when I learned how it feels to help somebody I like. And I realized something even simpler—that I could be a good friend to other people. I didn't know that before Lester."

The oval-face woman blotted her eyes with a tissue.

"I came away a better person because of Lester. It'll be hard to find another friend like him." He nodded to the audience. "But I'm going to try." Then he turned and took a final look inside the casket. The stick was right where he had put it. It had a ring of grease near the top from where the old man's hand had been so many times. Everything looked appropriate now.

THERE MUST have been ten or even fifteen people who came up to Alex and told him what a fine speech he had given. Rebecca's praise was the sweetest. She gave him a hug and said, "You did him proud, Alex. He'd feel so honored right now."

"Thanks," Alex said. He looked across the chapel and saw his mother exchanging business cards with a goateed man. She was doing what she did best. Networking.

He went over to the table in the front lounge and leaned over the registry. Dozens of people had written nice things about Lester. The book would be sent down to Earlene in Alabama. Alex could envision the old woman's hysterical tears saturating the pages.

He reached for the pen and flipped to the next page. "I liked your speech," someone said, directly behind him. It was a strangely familiar voice. "Very well done."

Alex turned around and could hardly believe what he saw. "No way," he said, dropping the pen. It was his father dressed in a black suit and black bowtie. "You were a true friend to him," he said.

Alex was too dumbfounded to give an intelligent response. He just stood there absorbing his father's presence.

"I thought it was time I paid you a visit." In place of his father's martini glass earring was a small diamond.

"I was just thinking about you," Alex finally said.

"Really?" He reached for Alex's shoulder. "Was it in a good way or bad?"

"Good," Alex said, still amazed by the sight of his father. "It was definitely good. But embarrassing."

"Tell me if you want." He pointed to the door. "How about we go outside for some air?"

Alex followed his father out the front door and down to the sidewalk. It was still cloudy, but no rain. They walked next to each other. Alex brought up the pain of losing Lester. "I've got this aching feeling that just sits right here." He pointed to the center of his chest.

"That's how it's supposed to be," his father said. "It'll get easier, less painful, but you'll never forget."

"Sounds like you've lost some people close to you."

"I have," his father said, "but this is Lester's day. Let it be his alone."

Until now, Alex had done a good job fending off his tears. But these words from his father caused him to cry. They walked a little while in silence.

Alex sniffled and said, "There's something I forgot to do. I forgot to thank you for paying Lester's fine...so thank you."

His father nodded. "You're certainly welcome."

"There's another thing too." As he walked, Alex looked down at the dividers in the sidewalk. "I'm sorry about missing the breakfast." The words came out with surprising ease.

"One thing about breakfast," his father said, "it happens everyday. But I appreciate your apology."

"And I'm sorry about leaving without saying goodbye."

"Apology accepted again," his father said. "You know, Alex, I never imagined you apologizing to me. It's always the other way around—me apologizing to you, for doing what I did, even for being who I am."

"You don't need to apologize for being gay," Alex said.

"You're right. It's not something I can control and therefore doesn't require an apology. But of all the people in the world, you're the one who's paid the greatest price."

Alex had a pretty good bullshit meter, and he could feel it firing away. "Being gay shouldn't be an excuse," he said, recalling Dale at the Days Inn and how that man never would have abandoned his child. "The biggest thing for me is that you weren't around all these years. I wish you would've been."